By the time the tour was over, Sara was thoroughly enchanted with the Rolling R ranch. On their way back to the house, the sun reached its zenith, beating down in heat waves.

"I knew today would be hot," Jackson said. "How're you holding up?"

"I'm a little tired." She was also light-headed, but didn't want to alarm him. Once her feet were on solid ground again, she'd be fine.

At last, they reached the stable. "Just sit tight," Jackson said, as he dismounted. "I'll help you down."

"I can manage." She gripped the saddle horn and stretched her leg over Lady Mary's rear end. As she slid to the ground, Jackson was there to meet her. Before she realized what was happening, he'd drawn her into his arms.

"Sara, I'm worried about you."

"Don't be," she said, although his concern touched her. "Like I said, I'm just tired."

Neither made a move to draw away. The longer they stood there, the more aware she became of how his arms steadied and sustained her. Being near him was dangerous, though. She should pull away, but her feet refused to move.

"We shouldn't have gone out today," he said. "The ride was too soon after your injuries."

"Please don't worry. I wanted to go. I had fun."

Shifting slightly, he drew back. Their gazes met. His was full of warmth and tenderness. Then tenderness deepened to desire and he leaned closer. His lips parted, his eyelids lowered as he focused on her mouth. "Sara," he said, ending her name with a groan.

Sara ran her tongue over her lips, and then closed her eyes and held her breath while his mouth gently covered hers.

Finding Sara

by

Linda Hope Lee

Finding Sara

Cover Art by *Kim Mendoza*

The Wild Rose Press
PO Box 708
Adams Basin, NY 14410-0706
Visit us at www.thewildrosepress.com

Publishing History
First Sweetheart Rose Edition, 2008
Print ISBN 1-60154-385-9

Published in the United States of America

Praise for Linda Hope Lee

On Tell Me No Lies:

"Well-written..fast-paced...highly recommended."
~Joyce Koehl, Romance Reviews Today

"Lee delivers another touching romance."
~Molly Charles, author of Chasing Galahad.

"An endearing and well-written romance. Highly recommended."
~Janalee, Love Romances.

"A town filled with secrets, a love story fraught with danger--my favorite kind of book."
~Stella Cameron,
New York Times bestselling author.

On Dark Memories:

"Pulsates with suspense."
~Gothic Journal

"Lee provides readers with emotional drama and puzzling suspense... .churns with guilt, passion, and intrigue."
~Romantic Times.

On Someone to Watch Over Me, a 2002 EPPIE finalist:

"A pleasing romance with just enough spice to satisfy readers." Romantic Times. "As romantic suspense stories go, this is one of the best."
~Scribes World.

"A fascinating, intriguing romantic suspense."
    ~Ivy Quill.

Chapter One

Sitting on a bench in the Red Rock, Colorado train station, Sara Carleton stared at the number on her cell phone's screen. Should she call her father or not? He'd still be angry, but he'd be worried, too. She should at least let him know she was all right. She punched the Send button and held the phone to her ear.

"Carleton residence," said a familiar voice.

As she'd expected, her father's household manager answered the call. "Hello, Foster, it's Sara."

"Miss Sara! Hold on. I'll get your father right away."

She pictured him, in his uniform of white shirt, black slacks and vest, hurrying off to summon his employer, J. Edward Carleton, III.

While she waited, Sara gazed around the train station. Red Rock was not her final destination. She'd begun her journey yesterday from her home in Long Island, New York, intending to travel across the country to California. Late this afternoon, the conductor announced a delay of several hours in Red Rock, while engine repairs were made.

Her gaze roved over the busy ticket counter, a café's arched doorway, and landed on a newsstand, where a man stood reading a newspaper. A brown cowboy hat hid most of his face, but his broad shoulders, lean waist, and long legs in hip-hugging jeans were in full view.

The man looked up, and, as though he'd known someone observed him, his gaze shot straight to her. Deep-set, dark eyes widened, and then narrowed in a sexy way.

A shiver of excitement sped down Sara's spine.

They continued to stare across the room, not even breaking contact when people passed between them. Although certain she'd never seen the man before, she had the craziest feeling she somehow knew him.

"Sara, where are you?"

Her father's deep voice, full of all the ferocity and indignation she had expected, jolted her. Reluctantly, she turned away from the cowboy. Keeping her voice calm, she said, "I just wanted to let you know I'm all right."

"Okay, but why did you take off without telling me you were leaving?"

"I think you know."

"The little discussion we had about your marrying Grayson?" He snorted. "You have bride's nerves. Very common and nothing to worry about."

Sara pursed her lips. He always presumed to know her feelings, while in truth, he hadn't a clue. "But—"

"You're having a wedding, and no more arguments!"

Aware of the hard bench underneath her, she shifted to a more comfortable position. Just the thought of marrying Grayson was enough to panic Sara. He was handsome and well mannered, but she wasn't in love with him. His kisses left her cold. She could go for days without seeing or talking to him and almost forget he existed.

No, her relationship with Grayson couldn't be love.

Her father didn't care about love. He dismissed the ten-year difference in their ages, insisting she and Grayson made a perfect match. He blatantly ignored her attempts to explain how she felt.

"Where are you?" her father queried. "We've already checked Palm Beach and Stowe, and no one's seen you."

After the last argument, desperation had sent her on the run. "I need to get away for a while."

"Fine. That's what the houses at Palm Beach and Stowe are for."

"Not to someplace I visit all the time. I mean, really away." She only hoped California would be far enough.

"Quit behaving like a rebellious teenager. You're twenty-two, and it's time to assume a woman's responsibilities. I've invested a great deal in you—nannies, tutors, private schools, trips to Europe. I even sent you to the gourmet cooking school you insisted on attending, although I thought it a waste of time for someone of your social position."

There he went again, laying on a guilt trip. When he wanted his way, he always dragged out his litany of all he'd done.

Anger exploded inside Sara, anger she wouldn't dare express were they face to face. "Yes, that's all I am to you, an investment! Just like your stocks and bonds, and your shopping malls."

"Now, Sara—"

Her fingers tightened on the phone. "Maybe I'll call you again sometime."

"What? Wait!"

"I'm hanging up now."

"Grayson and I will track you down! I know you didn't take any clothes. You'll leave a credit card trail. We'll find you!"

"Goodbye, Dad." Sara disconnected the call, turned off the phone, and tucked it into her purse. She heaved a deep sigh. Okay, she'd let him know she was all right. Now, she could continue her journey, although without a plan. She'd worry about that when the time came.

Remembering the handsome cowboy, Sara looked to see if he still stood at the newsstand.

He was there, but a woman with short, curly dark hair and toting a suitcase on wheels had joined him. Her hand rested on his arm and they bent their heads close together in conversation.

Sara sighed. He was taken, then. Well, so what? She had no intention of picking up a stranger, no matter how handsome and appealing.

Putting the cowboy out of her mind, Sara focused on her own situation. Her stomach growled and she glanced at her wristwatch. Eight o'clock. No wonder she was hungry. A bowl of soup and a sandwich sounded good. She rose from the bench and headed for the café.

As she crossed the station, she noticed some rough-looking men giving her the eye. She stuffed down a shiver and hurried past them.

Inside the café, a line of people waited for tables. She considered joining it, but when her stomach growled again, she knew she should eat something soon. Thinking she could surely find a restaurant close by, she turned and wove her way through the crowd to the nearest exit.

Sara stepped outside into a narrow alley between the station and another cement-walled building. To her left, the glow of neon beckoned. She headed toward the lights, but the farther she moved from the station, the darker the space became. A chill swept over her. Perhaps this wasn't such a great idea, after all. She should have stayed in the café and waited her turn for a table.

Halfway down the alley, she heard the sound of boots on asphalt and voices behind her. She glanced over her shoulder and saw three men. Other stranded travelers looking for a restaurant? She didn't think so. They looked more like the loiterers she'd noticed earlier. On instinct, she clutched the strap of her shoulder bag and quickened her steps. Just a few more yards and she'd be clear of the alley and out in the open.

The footsteps shuffled closer. Without stopping to look back, Sara broke into a run. She was no match for them, though, and soon they were directly behind her.

In the next instant, one grabbed her purse strap. Another jumped behind her and looped an arm around her neck. "Get it and let's get out of here!" yelled a third attacker from the sidelines.

No way. Her purse was her lifeline. Sara clawed at the arm around her neck while at the same time tugging on her purse strap.

"Give it up!" the man on the other end growled.

"No!" Sara kicked at his shin.

"You heard him. Drop it!" yelled the guy holding her by the throat.

"No!"

He jerked his arm against Sara's windpipe. Pain shot through her neck, radiating down her arms and her back. She choked and gasped for breath. With her breath cut off, her strength ebbed. The purse strap slipped through her fingers.

"Got it!" The robber waved his prize in the air.

The second attacker released her neck and shoved her toward the station wall. Her head slammed into the cement, and stars burst in front of her eyes. She barely had time to suck in a breath before crumpling to the ground.

Her attackers' footsteps faded into the night.

Then everything went black.

****

Jackson Phillips tucked his hand under his sister Rose's elbow and guided them across the train station. "How was your interview?" he asked. She'd been in Denver applying for a job as quality control manager with the railroad.

"It went really well," Rose said. "But, the current manager will be there for another month.

Even if I get the job, I won't report to work right away."

He gave her arm an affectionate squeeze. "I'll enjoy spending more time together. I've missed you."

A wry grin split her lips. "You missed my cooking, you mean."

Jackson chuckled at her accurate perception. "True, you're a fine substitute for Anna." Anna Gabraldi, his cook and housekeeper, was away visiting her ill daughter. "But, most of all, I missed your company."

"I know you did. But, oh, I hope I get the job! Cross your fingers for me, Jackson, will you?"

Jackson steered them around the long line snaking from the ticket counter. "Sure, Rose. I hope they hire you, since your heart's set on it." He wanted to sound enthusiastic, but knew there was a catch in his voice. If she were hired, Rose would be based in Denver, a couple hours' drive from Red Rock. The Rolling R would be a lonely place without her.

She cocked her head. "I'd still come home on my days off. But, Jackson, it's time for you to find someone. If you'd just open yourself up a little..."

A knot formed in Jackson's stomach. An entire year had passed since Cathleen's death. They would have been married by now, maybe with a baby on the way. Sometimes, the memories of her and the dreams they'd had hurt too much to bear. "I don't want to talk about my personal life."

She laid her head against his shoulder. "I'm sorry. I just hate to see you lonely and unhappy."

"Don't worry about me, Sis." He waved a hand. "Come on, let's take the back door to the parking lot."

Jackson and Rose stepped into the dark alley. "They should put more light out here," he complained.

Rose clutched his arm. "It is kind of creepy."

"I'm glad I came to meet you. Wouldn't want you out here by yourself."

"I'm glad you came, too... What's that up ahead?" Rose pointed into the darkness.

Jackson squinted and saw what appeared to be someone lying on the ground next to the train station wall. "Probably a drunk sleeping it off."

As they approached, light from the parking lot revealed a woman. She lay on her side, one arm under her, the other outstretched. Her eyes were closed, and strands of blond hair clotted with blood were plastered to her forehead.

Jackson gave a start. She was the woman who'd been making a cell phone call while he waited at the newsstand for Rose. The one who'd caught his eye when he'd casually looked up. He recalled the strange excitement he'd felt when they'd locked gazes.

How on earth had she ended up injured in the alley? He and Rose bent over the still body.

Rose placed her fingers under the woman's chin. "There's a pulse."

"We'll get help." Jackson pulled out his cell phone and punched 9-1-1.

Half an hour later, Jackson and Rose sat in the waiting room at Valley General Hospital. Rose paged through a magazine while Jackson stared at the beige walls and green upholstered furniture, his stomach churning. He'd spent far too much time in this building during Cathleen's illness.

Rose had insisted they come. The woman in the alley, apparently a mugging victim, had no purse or identification. No one in the station could be found who knew anything about her.

"We can't just leave her," Rose had said, as they'd watched the medics put the woman into their ambulance. "When she regains consciousness, she might need more help."

"Isn't there an organization to help stranded travelers?" he asked.

"Yes, there is, but we found her."

She sounded as though that gave them a proprietary claim on the injured woman. Rose was a natural caretaker, though, so Jackson really shouldn't have been surprised by her insistence. As a child, she'd always wanted to take in stray cats and dogs. Years later, after he'd bought the ranch and begun raising cattle and quarter horses, she'd nursed every sickly newborn calf or colt.

Jackson wasn't unsympathetic to the young woman's plight. Had he made the discovery alone, he'd probably be sitting here just the same.

But he sure hated being in this hospital. They'd told the ER receptionist they were waiting for word about the train station victim. So far, no news.

Another half-hour passed before the door to the examining rooms opened and Dr. Mike Mahoney appeared.

At the sight of his good friend, Jackson's spirits lifted. He and Mike had been buddies since they'd both played basketball at Red Rock High. With Mike on duty tonight, the injured woman was in capable hands.

Jackson jumped up. "Hey, Mike!"

"Jackson!" Mike's eyes lit up. "What are you doing here?"

In a few sentences, Jackson explained about finding the injured woman.

"Then you're who I'm looking for," Mike said. "I was told someone accompanied her."

"Yeah, Rose and I came." He nodded toward his sister.

Mike's gaze moved to Rose, who'd remained seated, partly hidden by Jackson, and a shadow crossed his face. "Hello, Rose," he said soberly.

8

"Hello, Mike." Rose darted him a glance, then lowered her eyelids.

Jackson sensed the tension between Rose and Mike. They'd been in a relationship until a few months ago when Rose broke it off. Jackson didn't know why, because neither wanted to talk about it. But, he'd always had the feeling they had unfinished business.

Now was not the time for Rose and Mike's problems. They were here to learn about the injured woman. "So, how is she?" he asked Mike.

"She has a concussion, and some bruises and lacerations, but she'll recover." Mike paused to shovel a hand through unruly reddish-brown hair.

"Find out who she is?" Jackson asked.

Mike shook his head and frowned. "No. She regained consciousness but doesn't remember her name or how she came to be at the station. Memory lapse is not unusual after a head injury, and, at this point, it's not something to worry about. We're keeping her overnight for observation."

Relieved to know he'd soon be leaving this uncomfortable place, Jackson nodded.

Mike pulled a clipboard from under his arm and consulted it. "She'll be in three thirty-one if you want to visit her."

"We do," Rose said, sitting forward and looking at Mike. "Jackson said they caught each other's eye in the station. Maybe seeing him again will jog her memory."

His encounter with the woman had been more than just a casual collision of glances. Even thinking about their looks now revived the shiver of excitement he'd experienced while they'd stared at each other across the crowded station. However, he'd downplayed the incident when relating it to Rose.

She turned to Jackson and laid her hand on his arm. "We can visit her, can't we?"

Jackson hesitated, looked at her expectant expression, and then said, "Sure."

However, as they headed toward the elevator, his gut feeling told him any further involvement with the injured woman would be trouble.

Chapter Two

A few minutes later, Jackson followed Rose into Room 331. The antiseptic smell reminded him once again of all the time he'd spent here, hoping against hope Cathleen would survive the cancer invading her young body. Sweat broke out on his forehead, and he wanted to turn and run.

Rose called out, "Hello! Hello!" and headed toward the train station victim, the only patient in the two-bed room.

He'd better follow along, or be prepared to answer Rose's questions later about his behavior. Yet, his step was hesitant as he crossed the room.

The woman turned her head in their direction. A faint smile curved her lips. "Hello. Do I know you?"

"Not yet. I'm Rose Phillips, and this is my brother, Jackson Phillips." She waved in Jackson's direction.

The woman shifted to focus on Jackson.

Would she remember him? He held his breath.

Her expression was blank.

Filled with a curious mixture of relief and disappointment, he exhaled.

"We're the ones who found you in the alley," Rose said. The woman turned her attention to Rose. "At a train station, the doctor said."

"Yes. Here in Red Rock."

As Rose went on to explain, Jackson studied the woman. A missing section of blond hair above her right ear exposed a ragged line of stitches. Her forehead, as well as her arms, sported cuts and purple bruises.

Looking beyond her injuries, he saw eyes a deep, vibrant blue, and a nose with a charming tilt. Her mouth, with its full lower lip, struck him as the most kissable pair of lips he'd ever seen.

Jackson's heart raced, just like when he'd seen her at the train station. What was going on here?

When Rose finished talking, he said, "Dr. Mike said you're having trouble remembering."

"Yes. It's really weird." She raised a hand and fingered the bruise on her forehead. Her nails were perfectly shaped ovals painted a pale pink.

"Jackson noticed you in the station." Rose shot him a glance over her shoulder. "Do you remember seeing him?"

The woman raised her eyebrows at Jackson. "You noticed me?"

"Yeah. I looked up from reading a newspaper and saw you talking on your cell. You looked around, too, and our gazes met." He shrugged, as though the incident had little importance. "When we found you in the alley, I recognized you."

She shook her head and winced. "I'm sorry, I don't remember you. I wish I did. Then maybe I'd know whom I was talking to on the phone. How kind of you to come to the hospital, though. Thank you."

"Is there anything we can do?" Rose asked.

"I wish you could tell me who I am!" Her brow puckered, as though she were about to cry.

Rose reached out and patted her arm. "It'll be okay. Memory lapses are common after a head injury like you've had."

"That's what the doctor said, but I feel so helpless."

"I bet everything comes back to you by morning," Jackson said.

"I hope so."

Leaving the hospital and the city of Red Rock behind, Jackson and Rose sped along the highway in his pickup. A bright moon lit up the blue-black sky and turned the road into a silver ribbon.

Jackson was just beginning to relax when he glanced at Rose and saw a furrowed brow he knew meant trouble. "I know what you're thinking," he said, "and it's a bad idea."

"But, Jackson, she has nowhere to go, and you have a big house—"

He raised his hand in protest. "Tomorrow her memory will return. She'll be on her way home— wherever that is."

Rose crossed her arms over her chest. "What if she doesn't get her memory back by tomorrow?"

"Her family will be looking for her. They'll find her."

"What if they don't?" she persisted. "What if she has no family?"

Jackson stiffened. "That's highly unlikely. But, even if she doesn't, she has friends. Everyone has someone who cares about them."

"But what if?"

"Rose, cut it out!" Irritation sharpened his tone. She was like a dog with a bone when she got her mind set on something.

Thankfully, she gave in and fell silent. Her retreat didn't keep him from thinking about the woman in the hospital, though. He saw that soulful gaze reaching out.

Intent on getting as far away as he could from Valley General Hospital and the injured victim in Room 331, he gripped the wheel and stepped on the gas.

****

"Don't you think we should look for Sara?" Grayson Delacourt asked.

J. Edward took another sip of port, savoring the taste of his favorite after-dinner drink. Then he set the glass on a mahogany end table and, in his best, no-nonsense tone, said, "No, I do not. She'll come running home tomorrow. You'll see."

Grayson wouldn't have known about Sara's unexpected absence, but the two had a date to attend a party tonight. When Grayson called for her half an hour earlier, J. Edward considered telling him she was ill and couldn't go out. In the end, he decided to be up front. After all, he and Grayson were allies.

Grayson's eyes narrowed. "How can you be sure she'll come home tomorrow? You said she has her credit cards."

J. Edward chuckled. "Sure, but she won't want to risk leaving a paper trail by using them. If she does get stubborn about coming home and makes some charges, then I'll cancel the cards."

"That could take awhile, though, couldn't it? I wish we knew where she was when she called."

"Unfortunately, I don't have the connections to trace a cell phone call."

"Did she say why she left?"

J. Edward pursed his lips. He hadn't anticipated all these questions. "Just a silly disagreement she and I had. She's impetuous, sometimes. You know how women are."

As J. Edward sipped his drink, he covertly studied Grayson over the rim of his glass. The other man's furrowed brow indicated he wasn't as casual about Sara's absence as he'd hoped.

Grayson said, "We should report her missing. She's already been gone the required twenty-four hours."

He waved away Grayson's concern. "That's not necessary."

"But she could be in trouble," Grayson protested.

"I assure you, she isn't. She's perfectly fine," J. Edward said through clenched teeth.

"But—"

J. Edward slammed down his glass on the end table. Liquor splashed over the rim, forming a shiny pool on the table's slick surface. He leveled a finger at Grayson. "Not a word of this to the police or to anyone, you understand? Neither of us needs any bad publicity right now. If anyone asks, she's at the Palm Beach house."

Grayson's nostrils flared, and his chest rose and fell in a deep breath. But then he said in a calm, controlled voice, "All right. But I'm worried, just the same."

"Don't be. Everything will turn out in our favor. You'll see."

"I hope so. Do we still have a deal?"

Ah, now he sounded downright apologetic. Just where J. Edward wanted him. "Of course, we do," he said. "We just have to get you two married to get the ball rolling."

After Grayson left, J. Edward poured himself another drink to replace the one he'd spilled. He eased back into his leather chair and stared out the window. Instead of seeing the courtyard with its burbling fountain and white, wrought iron furniture, his thoughts focused on Sara. He couldn't understand why she objected to marrying Grayson. He was well groomed, polite, and respectful. He treated her with the utmost courtesy and care. What more could she want?

His own arranged marriage had been successful. Although passion was lacking in the beginning, he and Ella grew to care deeply for each other. She'd been gone almost twenty years, and he still missed her. Over the years, he'd enjoyed the company of women, but he hadn't found anyone to take her place as his wife.

He doubted he ever would and had resigned himself to being single. Besides building a financial empire, he'd put all his efforts into raising his daughter. A daughter who had turned out to be very ungrateful and defiant, indeed.

****

As Grayson left the mansion and headed to his car, his stomach churned. Despite J. Edward's reasoning, he didn't share the older man's casual attitude about Sara's sudden absence. Why would she run off when there was so much to do for their upcoming wedding? He didn't like it. Not one bit.

He reached his sky blue Miata, unlocked the door, and slid onto the leather seat. He breathed deeply of the new car smell, to him every bit as aromatic as the smell of money. And, yes, he'd have more of that, too, once he and Sara were married.

But, he wasn't marrying her for only financial reasons. He loved her and wanted her to be his wife. How lucky he was to find both money and love. What a sweet deal.

This latest development raised a doubt about her feelings for him, though. What was she thinking? He'd done everything he could think of to make her fall in love with him.

He started the engine and took off down the drive toward the gatehouse. Good thing J. Edward hadn't made him promise not to look for Sara himself.

****

"You'll love the ranch," Rose said from the back seat of Jackson Phillips's SUV.

"I'm sure I will." Sara swallowed down her guilt and stared out the window as they left the hospital parking lot and headed for the freeway.

"You can relax and get your health back. And you're welcome to stay as long as you need to."

Rose chattered on, but Sara had trouble paying attention. She couldn't believe what had happened over the past two days. Train travel, a stop for repairs, a mugging, and an overnight hospital stay.

Following that, Jackson and Rose invited her to recuperate at Jackson's ranch. Not knowing what else to do, she'd agreed. Then, this afternoon, while she waited for them to pick her up, her memory suddenly returned. She recalled leaving the train station to search for a restaurant, the attack in the alley, and the theft of her purse.

Most important of all, she remembered why she had left home.

She'd opened her mouth to tell Rose and Jackson about her restored memory, but the words stuck in her throat. Without money or other resources, she would have to return home. Just the thought of facing her father—and Grayson—after running away made her want to throw up.

So, in the split second when a choice must be made, she decided to let everyone believe she still had amnesia. She would accept Rose and Jackson's generous invitation to stay at the ranch, but only until her injuries healed. Not more than a couple weeks, at most. By then, her stitches would have been removed and she'd be well enough to travel again. Money still would be a problem, but she'd figure something out when the time came.

She turned away from the traffic on Red Rock's Main Street to glance at Jackson. His cowboy hat was tipped back, offering a glimpse of curly black hair. His high forehead, bold nose, and firm chin made a distinctive profile.

Careful not to be obvious, she let her gaze slide down, over his muscular shoulders and broad chest. The rolled up sleeves of his denim shirt exposed strong wrists and arms sprinkled with dark hair. She sucked in a breath. The man positively reeked of sex appeal.

Again, she looked at his face, this time noticing the tight set of his mouth. He hadn't said much since they'd picked her up, offering only short answers or grunts to Rose's chatter.

The reason why hit her like a punch in the stomach—Jackson didn't want her on his ranch. Rose was the one who wanted to help her. Having Rose as an ally was a comfort, but Jackson's rejection hurt.

Was this charade a big mistake, even though for only a short time? Anxiety lumped in the pit of her stomach.

Rose tapped her on the shoulder. "Have you?"

Sara jerked and turned to look at the other woman. "I'm sorry. Have I what?"

"Thought of a name for yourself. Or do you want to be Jane Doe, like in the hospital?"

"I, ah, hadn't thought of another name, but I don't particularly care for Jane Doe, either." A twinge of guilt ran through her.

"Neither do I. But, until your memory returns, we have to call you something. Anything come to mind?"

Sara tensed. If she chose a name different from her true one, she might not respond when she heard it. "How about Sara?"

Rose grinned. "Good choice. 'Sara' suits you. What do you think, Jackson?"

"I suppose it'll do until she remembers her real name," Jackson said.

Now the name issue had been decided, Sara settled back into her seat. Still, she feared they would soon see through her pretense. Maybe she should tell the truth. Then she remembered her father's angry voice during their last argument. She thought of marrying Grayson. Nausea bubbled up inside her again.

No, she couldn't return home, and she couldn't marry Grayson.

But, although keeping her secret was the best choice, guilt lay on her shoulders like a heavy stone.

Sara didn't know what she expected of the Rolling R ranch. She'd been so wrapped up in her dilemma she hadn't thought much about Jackson's home. However, as soon as they passed under the arch with the name emblazoned in large wooden letters, and she saw only flat land punctuated here and there with clumps of trees, she realized the ranch was huge.

After passing fields of grain and a few meadows where cows grazed, they finally reached Jackson's house. The two-story, frame structure's rich brown color blended well with the landscape. A hanging swing and furniture made of logs filled the porch. Pots of red and orange geraniums lined the steps and the stone walk.

Like a picture postcard, the place charmed Sara. Furthermore, the house seemed to reach out and welcome her. Maybe the next couple of weeks would go smoothly, after all.

She glanced at Jackson again. At the sight of his grim mouth, the welcome feeling vanished like smoke, and a cold chill settled over her.

I'm an intruder here. I can't stay. I just can't.

Right now, what else could she do?

When Jackson pulled the SUV to a halt and he and Rose climbed out, Sara followed.

They entered through the back door, stepping into the kitchen. Furnishings included the usual sink, counters, cupboards, and appliances, plus a round maple table covered with a red-and-white checkered cloth.

"Come on, Sara," Rose said, "I'll take you up to your room."

Rose led her down a hallway, up a flight of stairs, and along another hall to a guest bedroom. A bed with a cheerful, yellow print spread dominated the room. Sheer yellow curtains adorned the windows and matching rag rugs accented the hardwood floor. The scents of fresh linen and furniture polish lingered in the air.

"This is a beautiful room," Sara began, and then her throat choked up. Even though she'd come this far, this arrangement wasn't going to work. "I–I can't stay here."

"Why not?" Rose opened one of the windows, and then turned to Sara. "Oh, I know losing your memory is upsetting. But don't worry, you'll get it back."

"It's not that..."

"What, then?"

Tears welled behind Sara's eyes. "Your brother doesn't want me here."

Rose stared. "Did he say that to you?"

"He didn't have to. I sensed his disapproval the whole way here."

Rose crossed the room and put a hand on Sara's shoulder. "I think I know why he's being standoffish. You see, Jackson lost his fiancée, Cathleen, a year ago. She became ill and passed away. And—"

"And I remind him of her?" Sara guessed, grateful for Rose's comforting gesture.

Eyes narrowed, Rose cocked her head. "No, I don't think that's it."

"Then what?"

"I'm not sure. He's a complicated man. But it's not you, personally. Trust me. I'm sorry he's sending out negative vibes, but I'm betting he'll soon relax and be friendlier. And remember, your stay here is short term."

Rose's reminder calmed Sara's fears once again. "Yes," she said, as much to herself as to Rose. "My stay here is only temporary."

Chapter Three

While Rose took Sara upstairs, Jackson paced the kitchen floor. He should check on the mare about to foal, and do other chores, but he knew he wouldn't be able to focus. He paused to rub the back of his stiff neck. His uptight feeling was Sara's fault, yet why was her presence here so distressing? Why couldn't he open his home to someone in need?

When he thought about it, the reason was obvious. He'd planned to bring Cathleen to the ranch after they were married. Cathleen should be settling in upstairs, not a stranger with amnesia.

Why had he let Rose rope and hogtie him into this?

Still, he had to admit part of his distress rested on his own shoulders. Since he'd seen Sara across the crowded train station, he'd been haunted by her image. Strange how he'd been glancing casually around and had focused on her. A few seconds either way and they'd never have noticed each other. If he and Rose had exited the front door instead of the back, they'd never have found Sara in the alley.

Even though he'd been madly, wildly in love with Cathleen and was in love with her memory still, Sara had turned his world upside down.

Get a grip. She'd soon be out of his life. Besides, she was Rose's project. Let Rose take care of her.
****
"You're leaving today?" Jackson stared at his sister then gazed into the mug of coffee he'd just poured when Rose dropped her bombshell. The aroma of eggs and bacon cooking on the stove under

her expert hand, moments ago so mouth watering, soured his stomach.

Rose flipped over an egg, then turned and nodded. "I'm afraid so."

He plunked his cup down on the table hard enough to slosh coffee onto the checkered cloth. "But you said even if you were hired, you wouldn't report for several weeks."

"I know, but Stan Doyle just called and said the current manager had a heart attack. He wants me to come right away." She looked at her wristwatch and frowned. "I have to hurry. I'm catching the eight-fifty train. You don't have drive me to the station. Molly is going into town for a check-up. Can you believe she's eight months pregnant already?"

Yes, Jackson knew his foreman Buck's wife was well along in her journey toward motherhood. "Don't try to distract me. What about her?" He pointed to the ceiling.

"She's still sleeping. I looked in on her before I came down." Rose scooped eggs and bacon onto a plate, added a couple pancakes from another skillet, and handed the plate to Jackson. "Here you go."

Staring at his food as if it were something foreign, he said, "I don't mean now, I mean later...after you're gone."

Rose's brow knit. "Are you talking about having to cook for her? Anna will be back this afternoon, won't she?"

"Yes, I'm expecting her. Cooking's not the problem." He gritted his teeth. "I don't want to have to entertain Sara. I have work to do."

"Sara doesn't need to be entertained. She needs to rest. Sit and eat, Jackson, before your food gets cold."

Grumbling, he pulled out a chair and sat. "How long will you be gone?"

"Don't know for sure." She picked up another

plate and served herself eggs and bacon. "Come on, you can handle this. Think about how much you're helping Sara. Don't you just glow inside?"

"Yeah. Glow." Jackson shoveled a forkful of eggs into his mouth and washed it down with orange juice.

Rose brought her plate to the table and joined him. She leaned over and put a hand on his shoulder. "You're wishing Cathleen had come here, aren't you? Not some stranger—"

"I never said that!"

"You didn't have to, dear brother. I know you very well. And I understand." She patted his shoulder. "Really, I do."

"This doesn't have anything to do with Cathleen," he said.

"All right, if you say so. But, you'll do just fine. When Sara has recovered her memory and is reunited with her loved ones, you'll have the satisfaction of helping someone who needed you."

By nine o'clock, Jackson paced the kitchen floor, waiting for Sara to come downstairs. Rose was long gone and on the train by now. She left in a flurry of good-byes and dust churned up by Molly's pickup. He put a plate of food in the oven to keep warm for Sara then cleaned up the dirty dishes.

Although Buck and the crew all were capable, Jackson needed to be out working. But he didn't want to leave without first seeing Sara. If she came down and found no one, she'd wonder what was going on. He glanced at the notepad by the telephone. He could leave her a note, but he'd feel better if he talked to her in person.

He was about to stomp up the stairs and bang on her door when the floor overhead creaked and the pipes hummed with running water. Okay, she was underway. He poured himself another cup of coffee and sat at the table. The thought of seeing her again kept his nerves thrumming.

At last, footsteps sounded on the stairs. He jumped up and busied himself at the sink. He didn't want her to think he was sitting around waiting for her to put in an appearance, even if it were true.

"Good morning," she said when she entered the kitchen.

With an effort, he pasted on a smile and turned. "Oh, hi, there."

She wore a blue T-shirt and jeans—Rose's, of course. She and Rose weren't quite the same size, and the jeans were a little large. Still, they fit well enough to outline her long legs.

With blond hair pulled into a ponytail and face bare of makeup, Sara appeared young and vulnerable. Dark eyelashes provided a dramatic frame for deep blue eyes, and her lips were a natural pink. His chest ached. Her mouth was certainly made for kissing.

He took a deep breath and gestured to the coffeemaker. "How 'bout a cup of coffee?"

She smiled. "Just what I need."

He poured coffee into a mug and, not wanting to risk touching her, placed it on the table for her to pick up.

Sara looked around while she sipped her coffee. "Where's Rose?"

"She had to go to Denver."

A frown puckered her brow. "Oh. Will she be back soon?"

"'Fraid not." He explained about Rose's new job with the railroad.

Sara said nothing, but her eyes widened.

He could almost hear the wheels in her mind turning over this new twist of events. "Are you ready for something to eat?" he asked. "Rose made pancakes, bacon, and eggs before she left." He grinned. "Which is lucky for you, because I'm not much of a cook."

"Whatever Rose fixed will be fine. Is it on the stove?"

"There's a plate in the oven. I'll get it." He took a step toward the stove.

She held up a hand. "I can serve myself. You don't have to stick around, either. I know you must have a lot to do."

Jackson stopped and shoved hands into his jeans pockets. "Yeah, I do. But I want to make sure you get something to eat and are set for the day." That wasn't the only reason. He wanted to spend time with her, too.

"I appreciate that."

He watched Sara dish up her food and sit at the table, then ambled over to join her. Her plate held one lone pancake and a small mound of eggs. "Not much of a breakfast."

"I'm not very hungry." She picked up her fork and poked half-heartedly at the eggs.

Rose's sudden absence must really be bothering her. Maybe having company today would help to ease her discomfort. "Our housekeeper, Anna Gabraldi, will be here this afternoon to clean and cook dinner," he volunteered.

She looked up, her eyes brightening. "Oh. Does she...live here?"

"No, but she comes every day. For the past two weeks, she's been visiting her sick daughter." He sipped his coffee. "She's supposed to be back today."

"I see." She lowered her eyelids.

Realization dawned. Her discomfort went deeper than just having company during the day. The subject had been in his thoughts, too. Bringing it out in the open might put both their minds at ease.

"If you're worried about staying here alone with me, don't. I won't—I mean, you're safe."

Sara's cheeks turned pink.

Oh, hell, he should've planned exactly what to say before opening his big mouth. But he didn't want her to think that just because they were alone now, he'd make a move.

"I know what you're trying to say," she said, but continued to look downcast.

"What's wrong, then?"

She shifted in her seat. "I don't want to be a burden on you, or on Rose. I hate imposing."

"Well, I gotta admit, this was all Rose's idea."

"I know," she murmured. Then she straightened and in a firmer tone, said, "Look, why don't you take me back to Red Rock? I'm sure I can find someplace to stay until I get my stitches out. Maybe there's an agency that helps stranded travelers."

"I'm sure there is." He leaned his elbows on the table. "But you're here now, so you might as well stay to rest and recuperate. Besides, you'll be getting your memory back any day."

Sara stared at her plate. "Yes, my memory is the key to everything, isn't it?"

After Sara finished eating, Jackson gave her a tour of the house. Last night, she'd seen the living room and glimpsed some of the other rooms. Today he wanted to focus on things she might do while he was gone, such as watch a movie from his extensive DVD collection or read a book from his library. He also wrote down his cell phone number. "Don't hesitate to call if something comes up."

When the tour was over, they returned to the kitchen. Sara crossed to the screen door and gazed out. "Looks like you have a garden," she commented.

"We raise a few vegetables, corn and peas, and tomatoes. Having really fresh food is a treat."

He had come up behind her, and for one crazy moment, he had the urge to reach out and rest his hands on her shoulders, like he used to do with Cathleen. Then he would lean down and nuzzle her neck, rubbing his lips over her warm skin.

Would Sara's skin be warm, too? Just thinking about touching her made his fingers itch to find out.

Hey, man, stop that. He stepped back and shook his head to clear such notions. He wasn't interested in Sara. Besides, hadn't he assured her she was safe here? He took a deep breath, and then said, "If you feel like stretching your legs, take a walk. There's a pond and ducks beyond the garden. Bingo will keep you company." He pointed to his brown-and-white collie lying under an apple tree. "Here, boy!"

The dog stood, shook himself, and trotted over.

Jackson leaned around Sara and opened the door, and Bingo ambled in. "This is Sara." He patted Bingo's head, and then ran his hand down the animal's silky back. "You can be her pal today."

"Hello, Bingo." Sara held out her fist for the dog to inspect.

Jackson watched the two, feeling better now about leaving her. Yet, he couldn't seem to tear himself away. "Are you sure you'll be okay?"

A smile flashed and she nodded. "I'll be fine. Really. Go already."

****

As soon as Jackson left, Sara closed the back door and leaned against it, exhaling a sigh of relief. The constant worry she'd slip and give herself away kept her nerves on edge. Rose had been right, though. Jackson was friendlier this morning, as if making up for yesterday's aloofness. And, when she gave him the opportunity to take her back to Red Rock, he refused. Then he must be okay with her staying.

His reassurance about her safety around him gave her a smile, yet she was glad he'd brought up the subject. In truth, the idea had made her uncomfortable. Knowing he didn't want to get involved any more than she did helped her to accept

27

the situation.

Under other circumstances, she might feel differently. The man was quite handsome. She imagined putting her arms around him and running her hands down his back, over his firm muscles...and then kissing him.

What would his lips feel like on hers? Cold and dry, like Grayson's? She didn't think so. Her cheeks warmed.

Don't go there. Not even for a minute.

Sara sighed and forced her mind back to the present. She cleaned up her breakfast dishes and started the dishwasher, something she never did at home, and which gave her a curious feeling of independence and accomplishment. Then, needing some fresh air, she called to Bingo.

The dog jumped up from his blanket in the corner and followed her out the back door.

Midmorning sun graced a cloudless sky. Aromas of hay and grass drifted on the light breeze, and a cow's soft "moo" echoed in the distance.

With Bingo at her heels, Sara headed down a path leading to a barn. She was tempted to go inside, but the sunshine heating her skin was a stronger pull. She'd have time later to see the horses.

The duck pond Jackson mentioned had a wire dome to keep out predators. The ducks, snowy white against the dark water, glided about as though they hadn't a care in the world.

If only I could be so at peace.

She sat on a wooden bench, hoping to relax and enjoy the morning. But her troubles wouldn't leave her alone. How long would she stay here, and where would she go when she left?

After lunch, Sara's head started to ache, as the doctor warned. She took a couple of aspirin and curled up under a blanket on the living room's leather sofa. Eventually, she drifted off to sleep.

The telephone's ring jolted her awake. Remembering Jackson had said the answering machine would pick up messages, she settled back down.

Jackson's recorded voice asked the caller to leave a message, then a woman said, "Jackson, this is Anna. I have some bad news. My daughter's recovered, but now her mother-in-law is sick, and my daughter and her husband are going to Georgia to visit her. I'll be caring for the grandkids. Don't know how long they'll be gone. I called a few of my friends to see if someone could fill in at your place—I know how you hate to cook—but no luck. Sorry to leave you in the lurch. I'll call again when I have an update."

A click indicated Anna had hung up.

A moment passed before the woman's message registered on Sara. "Oh, no." She clutched the blanket to her chest. Now, no one would provide a buffer even part of the time between her and Jackson. Bad news indeed.

She stared at the high-beamed ceiling. Why had this happened? If only the train hadn't stopped in Red Rock, she'd be in California by now, enjoying independence from her father and Grayson.

She didn't want to sit around feeling sorry for herself. Her Grandmother Millie, who had helped to raise her, always said the best remedy for "a case of the blues" was to get busy and do something.

But what could Sara do here? She thought about the phone message from Anna Gabraldi. Jackson expected her to arrive today and cook the evening's meal. Now, Anna wouldn't be coming.

An idea popped into Sara's mind. She sat up and threw back the blanket, then rose and marched into the kitchen.

29

Chapter Four

At five o'clock, Jackson returned to the ranch house. In the barn, he unsaddled and brushed his horse, Domino. He patted him on the nose and checked the amount of hay in the manger. Then he picked up the saddle and bridle and carried them into the tack room.

Before leaving, he fed the other horses, including Jenny, the mare about to foal. A rich mahogany color and with a long, sleek neck, she was one of his finest quarter horses. Her belly hung round and heavy. Soon there would be a new colt to care for. Jackson smiled to himself. Raising horses gave him great pleasure.

He left the building, securing the door behind him. The day out on the range had been fulfilling. He'd relished the open space, the fresh air, and the warmth of the sun. He'd eaten lunch in the bunkhouse dining room with the ranch hands, joining in their banter. Afterward, he and Buck discussed their next grain order and how to fix a broken tractor.

Now the day was over, and he had to face Sara again, the beautiful stranger with golden hair and deep blue eyes. The image of her sitting at his kitchen table eating breakfast popped into his mind.

Sara would be at the house waiting. They'd have dinner together, spend the evening together. His gut tightened. If any woman waited, she should have been Cathleen, not this troublesome stranger thrust upon him by circumstance.

Then he remembered Anna would be there, too.

He squared his shoulders and lifted his chin. What lay ahead wouldn't be so bad after all. Anna was a friendly, talkative soul, and she'd keep the conversation going.

And he really liked her cooking.

True to his expectation, as he approached the house, a tempting aroma drifted from the kitchen. Jackson quickened his steps, opened the screened door and stepped inside, ready to greet Anna.

He saw only Sara instead. Her back to him, she stood at the stove, stirring something in a large pot. Helpless to stop himself, his gaze traced her outline, from the golden hair curling about her slim shoulders, to her slender waist, to her long, elegant legs. He swallowed hard. She sure made a pretty picture.

At the sound of the door opening, she turned. "Hey, Jackson."

Her smile sent his heart into overdrive. "Hello, Sara." Jackson took off his hat and hung it on the coat rack. "Where's Anna?"

Sara's brow wrinkled. "She's not coming. Her son-in-law's mother is ill. The message is on your machine. The volume was turned up and I heard her call."

No Anna? Jackson's shoulders tensed.

After exchanging boots for indoor tennis shoes, he went into the living room and listened to Anna's call. Not only was she not coming today, her absence sounded indefinite.

She wasn't at fault, though. Things happened, and he was sorry there was more sickness in her family. He took a few deep breaths to calm down, and returned to the kitchen.

Sara was still tending the pot on the stove.

"So, you're cooking dinner," he said, then felt dumb for stating an obvious fact.

"I hope you don't mind?"

"Well, no. But you didn't have to."

She picked up a saltshaker and shook it over the pot. "I know that. But I heard Anna say you don't like to cook. And I remembered you said so this morning, too."

Jackson propped his hands on his hips. "Right, but we could've headed into town for a bite. Red Rock has several good restaurants."

"Fixing dinner was something to do. Besides, I like to cook."

He raised his eyebrows. "You do? You've remembered something, then?"

Her cheeks reddened. "Not exactly. Cooking just seemed to, ah, come naturally. A woman knowing how to cook is not unusual."

"I suppose not. But what about your dizzy spells? Did you have any today?"

Sara returned to her stirring. "Thankfully, no. I had a headache earlier, but aspirin and a nap chased it away."

"Good to hear. You'd better be careful over the hot stove, though. What are you making, anyway?" He crossed to the stove. When he leaned over the pot, his arm brushed Sara's.

They both jumped in opposite directions. The spoon in her hand flipped out of the pot and splattered red sauce on the white enameled stovetop.

"Oh, no! Look at the mess." She grabbed a washcloth from the sink and swiped at the stains.

"Sorry!" He'd been so interested in what she was cooking he'd forgotten he wanted to keep his distance. Too late now. The accidental touch left him breathless.

He grabbed a paper towel to help her clean up, but she'd already finished and had the spoon back in the pot.

Her face was flushed and tendrils of damp hair curled around her delicate ears. The urge was strong

32

to reach out and touch her hair, to see if it was as silky as it appeared.

Instead, he clasped his hands behind his back and focused on the contents of the pot. "Smells good. What is it?"

"A sauce for the chicken. I found some fryer parts in the freezer and thawed them in the microwave."

"Chicken?" He glanced at the stove. "I don't see any chicken."

"It's baking in the oven. I'm ready to pour the sauce over it now."

"What kind of sauce?"

"Tomato base and a few spices. Not all the ones I wanted, though. I couldn't find many in your cupboard."

"That's because I'm mainly a meat-and-potatoes man."

She lowered her eyelids. "Oh, sorry. I didn't know..."

Realizing he'd hurt her feelings, he waved a hand. "I'm sure whatever you've made will be fine." Jackson stood back while she opened the oven door and removed a steaming pan of chicken.

She set it on the stove, picked up the pot, and ladled the sauce over the chicken.

The spicy aroma made his stomach rumble.

She said over her shoulder, "Why don't you do whatever you usually do when you come in for dinner? Just pretend I'm Anna."

His gaze roved over Sara's lithe figure and blonde hair. Pretend she was Anna. Yeah, right. The idea made him laugh out loud. "No offence to Anna," he said, "but you two are opposites. She's in her sixties, at least thirty pounds heavier, and she wears her gray hair in a topknot. No way can I stretch my imagination that far."

"I see what you mean." She laughed, too, easing

the tension between them.

"I will get out of your way, though." Jackson went to the living room, sat in his favorite leather recliner, and switched on the TV. He tuned in the evening news, but not a word sank into his brain. He kept thinking of Sara in the kitchen, cooking his dinner.

Twenty minutes later, Sara set the chicken casserole on the table. She took a last look at everything: the basket of biscuits made from a premix she'd found, the plate of pasta, the bowls of peas and tossed salad. Not too bad a menu for spur-of-the-moment. She went to the door of the living room.

Jackson sat in a leather easy chair, his feet propped up on a footstool, watching the news.

"Dinner's ready," she called, then returned to the kitchen and sat at the table. With a shaky hand, she unfolded her napkin and spread it on her lap. Although cooking had lifted her spirits, now, she'd have to sit across the table from him and eat the meal she'd prepared. Even though she felt better about being here with Jackson in the house, what would she do now that Anna was not coming? Sara twisted her napkin into a knot.

The TV clicked off, and Jackson came in and sat across from her.

The round table seemed to shrink. She could easily reach out and touch his arm, run her fingers along the corded muscles, over the light sprinkling of dark hair. She shoved away those thoughts and concentrated on passing him the pasta.

"Everything tastes great," Jackson said after he had sampled the food.

"Thanks." A little thrill rippled down her spine. Then, remembering his earlier remark about liking meat and potatoes, she wondered if he really meant the compliment or was only being polite.

They ate in silence for a few minutes then he said, "You know, you might have a husband somewhere, and maybe children. Did you ever think about that?"

"No, I haven't," she said, thankful she could answer without lying. The only worry was the husband she might end up with, if she returned home.

Seeing Jackson's raised eyebrows, she added, "I mean, I've been preoccupied with the trauma of what happened. The head injury, having my identity and money taken away."

"Yes, of course," he said. "But, if you do have a husband, I'm sure he's doing everything possible to find you. I would, if you were my wife."

Seizing the opportunity to turn the discussion in his direction, she asked, "Have you ever been married?"

A shadow crossed his face. "No."

Oh, dear, he must be thinking of Cathleen. She wished she could take back the question. The subject of marriage and children had put them both in a funk.

For the remainder of the meal, they kept the conversation on more general topics. Still, Sara's nerves were on edge, and when Jackson brought the coffee pot to the table and motioned to her cup, she shook her head. "No, thanks. Why don't you enjoy your coffee in the living room while I clean up?"

"I'll help you."

"Thanks, but I'd rather work alone." She needed to be away from him for a while. "You've been so kind and my helping out would be a way to pay you back."

His brows knit. "I don't need to be repaid."

"Take it as a simple thank you, then." Why was he so touchy? She rose, picked up their empty plates and, conscious of his gaze on her back, carried them to the sink. She held her breath, wondering what he would say next to challenge her.

However, the only sounds were his footsteps as he crossed the kitchen and went into the living room. Seconds later, the television rumbled on.

At the amplified sound, she took a deep breath and sagged against the counter. What a relief to finally be alone. Having him around kept her nerves strung like a tightrope. She was afraid to say much, afraid she'd slip up and he'd figure out her memory had returned. She feared he'd be furious. No matter how polite and helpful he'd been today, the bottom line was, he resented her presence.

Maybe he just preferred to be alone.

She shook her head. Rose had been living there. And, he'd been quite happy to learn Anna was returning.

More likely, his fiancée, Cathleen, was the cause. He wishes she were here, instead of me.

He must have loved Cathleen very much. And for a moment, even though irrational, she resented Jackson's former fiancée. She wished with all her heart that she were far away from the Rolling R ranch and Jackson Phillips. How would she ever get through even the rest of this evening, much less the days and, heaven forbid, the weeks ahead?

Spending the evening alone with Jackson was easier than Sara had thought. The television came to her rescue. Like a third person, it chattered away, making conversation between her and Jackson unnecessary. They watched the news and shared a few laughs over a couple of sitcoms.

However, at nine thirty, a heavy silence greeted Sara's announcement that she'd better go to bed.

"Sure, go on," he finally said. "I'll stay down here and read awhile." He snatched up the newspaper and ducked behind it.

Sara climbed the stairs to her bedroom. She

shut the door, blocking out the sounds of the TV, and then undressed and put on a pair of Rose's cotton pajamas. Opening the door, she peeked out, hoping he wouldn't come along just as she headed for the bathroom.

The hallway was clear. Sounds of the TV floated up the stairs, indicating he was still there. She scooted across the carpet to the bathroom. On the way back, she risked a glance along the hallway. All the rooms had their doors shut. She wondered which one was his. The farther away he was, the better.

With a sigh, she entered her room and shut the door. For a moment, her fingers lingered on the lock then she pulled away. Jackson wouldn't barge in and force himself on her. No, he was an honorable man. Of that, she was sure.

She climbed into bed and settled under the covers. The bed was comfortable, if not as big as her canopied one at home. And the cotton, rather than silk, sheets were just as smooth. She took a deep breath and noticed a fresh air scent her silk ones lacked. With a wiggle, she crossed her arms over her stomach and prepared for sleep.

Half an hour later, after she'd changed her position at least twenty times, she was about to fall asleep at last. Just then, the stairs creaked. She tensed and her eyes flew open. Jackson coming up to bed. Okay, so what? The man had to sleep sometime, didn't he?

Still, her heart pounded like a jackhammer. The footsteps came down the hall, closer and closer. She held her breath, waiting to hear if he would stop outside her door.

And what if he did?

Don't be silly! She had nothing to fear.

Sure enough, he continued on down the hall without missing a beat. Then the sound of a door opening and closing. After that, all was quiet.

Sara rolled over and punched up her pillow. This arrangement just wasn't going to work. Tomorrow she would figure out a way to be on her own again.

****

The following morning, Jackson sat at the kitchen table, his first cup of coffee, which he usually relished, all but forgotten. He was watching Sara reach up to take a bowl from the cupboard. Morning sunlight outlined the curve of her cheek and edged her eyelashes with gold. Today she wore another of Rose's shirts, this one of denim, with tiny rosebuds decorating the collar. He'd given it to his sister for her birthday and always thought it flattered her. The shirt looked great on Sara, too.

She'd gathered her hair in a ponytail again, exposing her delicate ears. Stud earrings looked like real diamonds, although he couldn't tell for sure. To make that judgment, he'd have to get a lot closer than comfort allowed.

He noticed she'd removed all the pink polish from her fingernails. He liked her nails their natural shade. Cathleen had rarely worn nail polish, except for special occasions, such as Christmas and New Year's, and then she'd chosen clear, rather than colored.

"Jackson?"

Her voice jolted him back to awareness. "Huh?"

"I asked how you like your eggs."

"Oh." He cleared his throat, pushing away his guilt over comparing the two women. "Over easy, yolks about half done. You sure you want to cook again?"

"Yes, really." She straightened, a frown wrinkling her brow. "You don't mind, do you? Did I pass muster last night?"

"You sure did." Cooking apparently made her happy, so why not let her continue?

He waited until she'd pulled a carton of eggs

from the refrigerator, and then said, "I thought you might like a tour of the ranch this morning."

She turned and smiled, but then a hairline frown creased her forehead. "Don't you have work to do?"

"Always. Running a ranch is a fulltime job. But today is Saturday, and I try to take some time off on the weekends. A holdover from my nine-to-five days, I guess."

Sara cracked an egg and slid it into the skillet. Grease sizzled. "So you haven't always been a rancher?"

Her interest pleased him. "No. I grew up in Red Rock and went to Denver U. After I graduated, I worked as a broker on Wall Street."

"What happened?"

"I found out big city life wasn't for me. Those tall buildings were like a prison. I got lucky with my investments, and when I was ready to leave, I had enough to buy this spread."

She shot him a grin. "I'll bet more than luck was involved."

He nodded. "Okay, so I'm good at picking winners. But, success in the stock market is a lot of luck, too."

"And you're happier here?"

"Much happier. Except..."

"What?" Sara deftly flipped over the eggs.

He'd been about to comment on the loneliness but changed his mind. "Nothing. We got way off the subject. I asked if you wanted to see the ranch."

"I would. Very much."

"Best way is on horseback."

"Fine."

Wow, that was easy. "No qualms about riding? Maybe you know how."

She dropped the pancake turner, then ducked down and snatched it up. "I, ah, we'll see, won't we?"

Chapter Five

Later, wearing a pair of Rose's boots and one of her cowgirl hats, Sara followed Jackson out to the stable. Misgivings kept her stomach tied in knots. When he'd asked if she wanted to see the ranch, she'd jumped at the chance. True, she'd vowed that today she'd find a way to be on her own. So far, though, she didn't have a clue how. Maybe something would come to her if she relaxed rather than pressured herself.

When he'd mentioned riding, she'd almost let slip she knew how to ride. Of course, she knew. Every young woman in her social circle had been put on a horse at the earliest possible age. Sara had been three and she'd had riding lessons for years. Her horse, Marco, was kept in a private stable not far from the Carleton's Long Island home.

Today, she'd have to work hard to keep all her experience a secret.

They passed the vegetable garden where corn stalks towered over tomato plants and pea vines. At Jackson's call, Bingo roused himself from under the apple tree and joined them.

When they reached the stable, Jackson opened the door and they stepped inside. The familiar smells of horses, hay, and leather reminded her more than ever of home. For one brief instant, she wished she were back in New York, coming to get Marco, instead of here in Colorado, getting ready to ride Jackson's horse.

I'll come back for you someday, Marco. Don't you worry.

"I have the perfect horse for you." Jackson led Sara down the row of stalls to one occupied by a horse with a reddish-brown coat. "Meet Lady Mary."

Sara reached out to pat the animal's silky nose. "She's beautiful."

"Yes, and she's a gentle mount. Even if you've never ridden, I'll bet you're a quick study."

"I hope so."

He turned and gestured to a horse across the way. "I'll take Domino. He's my favorite. As soon as they're saddled, we'll be on our way."

"Can I help?"

His eyebrows shot up. "Sure, if you want."

Sara followed Jackson to the tack room. After he picked out the saddles and bridles he wanted, they carried them to the center of the stable. Then he brought out each horse separately to be outfitted.

She stood to one side, unable to ignore how his muscles strained against his shirt as he bent over to adjust the strap under Lady Mary's belly. Her breath quickened. He sure was a sexy man.

After the horses were ready, they led them outside into the sunshine. Of course, Sara could've mounted Lady Mary on her own, but she dutifully listened to Jackson's instructions.

"Grab the saddle horn," he said, "and slip your left foot into the stirrup."

Sara obeyed, impressed by his patience with a novice.

"Now put your right foot into my hands." He laced his fingers together and held them out.

Resting her hand on his shoulder, she again followed his direction.

As he lifted her up, his warm breath fanned the back of her neck, sending little tingles down her spine.

"Swing your right foot over. There. Good job!"

"Thanks." She smiled down from her position in

the saddle.

Jackson mounted Domino, and after his demonstration on how to hold the reins, they rode off, Bingo trotting alongside.

A cool morning breeze drifted down from the hills, while the sun climbing the cloudless sky promised a warm afternoon. The rich smell of the earth tickled Sara's nose. Birds sitting on fence railings twittered and chirped as they passed by.

Presently, they came to fields spread out on both sides of the road—some brown and bare, others green with new growth.

"It's hay," he told her. "Although my main business is raising quarter horses, I have a few cows, too. They're in the upper pasture. We'll go there another time."

He showed her the track where the horses were trained, a huge, fenced area where deep ruts in the ground marked countless hours of horse and rider sessions.

"Some are trained for working," Jackson said. "Others for show, and, depending on their temperament, for rodeo. My trainer's not here today," he added. "I'm not the only breeder he works for, so he lives in town."

Sara listened politely as he talked about life on the ranch.

After awhile, he paused and looked over. "So, does what I've told you ring any bells? Think you've been on a ranch before?"

"Everything sounds new to me," she said, glad to be able to give a truthful answer.

He took them down a side road leading to a group of buildings. "This is where my crew lives."

She looked at the wooden structures. "How many employees do you have?"

"Five. My foreman, Buck, and his wife, Molly, live in the small green house. Sandy, Phil, and Diego

stay in the bunkhouse next door. Here's Buck now."
Jackson nodded at a tall, long-legged man emerging
from a barn. "Hey, Buck!"

The man smiled and strode toward them.
"Jackson. Didn't expect to see you this mornin'."

"I'm showing Sara around." Jackson turned to
Sara. "I told Buck and Molly and the others about
you and your memory loss. Hope you don't mind."

Oh, great, more people she'd have to be careful
around. But she smiled and nodded to Buck.
"Pleased to meet you."

"Likewise." Buck tipped his hat, revealing
straw-colored hair and features that were pleasantly
boyish.

"You get the tractor fixed yet?" Jackson asked.

"No, but I figured out the problem." Buck held
up a twisted piece of metal. "I'm goin' into town to
get a new part."

"We're making sure all our equipment is ready
for cutting the hay later on this summer," Jackson
explained to Sara.

The creak of a door opening drew Sara's
attention to the green house. A young woman
stepped out onto the porch. A yellow cotton smock
stretched over her very pregnant stomach. Her red
hair was as shiny as a new penny, and a sprinkling
of matching freckles danced across her upturned
nose.

Buck leaped to lend her a hand down the steps.
"Careful, honey."

"Thanks, dear." The two exchanged a look full of
warmth and love.

Sara couldn't help being envious. Would she
ever know the joy of a loving relationship, as well as
of motherhood?

Jackson and Molly greeted each other, and then
Jackson gestured to Sara. "Meet Sara, the woman I
told you about."

"Hello." Molly shaded her eyes as she looked up at Sara. "I hear you had a terrible experience at the train station."

Sara rubbed her head wound, wincing at the stiffness of the stitches under her fingers. "I did. But I'm getting better."

"They catch the muggers?" Molly asked, while Jackson and Buck continued their conversation about the tractor.

"Not that we've heard."

"Jackson said you lost your memory."

As Lady Mary took a step forward, Sara shifted in the saddle. "I did, yes." Not exactly a lie. She had lost her memory—for a while.

Molly shook her head. "I can't imagine what that would be like."

"Very frustrating." Again, true. Still, the topic made her uncomfortable. "When's your baby due?"

"In about six weeks." Molly smoothed her smock over her stomach, green eyes gleaming with pride. "It's our first."

Just then, Jackson and Buck finished their conversation.

Molly asked, "Would you two like to come in for a cup of tea or coffee?"

Jackson shook his head. "Maybe some other time. I want to finish showing Sara around before the temperature drives us back indoors."

"Come visit me any time you get lonesome," Molly told Sara.

"Thanks. I'd like that."

"They're really nice," Sara commented as she and Jackson rode off. She especially liked Molly. The young woman was more down-to-earth than her socialite friends on Long Island.

Jackson nodded. "They're my good friends as well as employees."

"They seem so happy."

"They are. They're lucky to have found each other."

Hearing his wistful tone, Sara wished she hadn't made the comment. Relationships were a touchy subject for both of them. "Tell me more about your ranch."

By the time the tour was over, Sara was thoroughly enchanted with the Rolling R ranch. On their way back to the house, the sun reached its zenith, beating down in heat waves.

"I knew today would be hot," Jackson said. "How're you holding up?"

"I'm a little tired." She was also light-headed, but didn't want to alarm him. Once her feet were on solid ground again, she'd be fine.

At last, they reached the stable. "Just sit tight," Jackson said, as he dismounted. "I'll help you down."

"I can manage." She gripped the saddle horn and stretched her leg over Lady Mary's rear end. As she slid to the ground, Jackson was there to meet her. Before she realized what was happening, he'd drawn her into his arms.

"Sara, I'm worried about you."

"Don't be," she said, although his concern touched her. "Like I said, I'm just tired."

Neither made a move to draw away. The longer they stood there, the more aware she became of how his arms steadied and sustained her. Being near him was dangerous, though. She should pull away, but her feet refused to move.

"We shouldn't have gone out today," he said. "The ride was too soon after your injuries."

"Please don't worry. I wanted to go. I had fun."

Shifting slightly, he drew back. Their gazes met. His was full of warmth and tenderness. Then tenderness deepened to desire and he leaned closer. His lips parted, his eyelids lowered as he focused on her mouth. "Sara," he said, ending her name with a groan.

Sara ran her tongue over her lips, and then closed her eyes and held her breath while his mouth gently covered hers. His warm lips sparked a heat that surged through her like wildfire. Her knees trembled, and her pulse raced. If he hadn't been holding her, she would have crumpled to the ground.

Uncurling her arms from against his chest, she wrapped them around him, pulling him tight. Jackson's lips slid back and forth over hers. The sweet taste of him thrilled her to the core. She lost all track of time and place as he spun her through space on a merry-go-round of pleasure.

Leaving the clouds behind, she was headed for the stars when one of the horses gave a loud whinny. Like guilty children, Sara and Jackson jumped apart.

"I'd better see to the horses," he mumbled.

In a daze, Sara ran a finger over her lips, still warm from his kiss. "I'll help you."

"No, you're going into the house. I'll tend the horses." His mouth settled into a grim line.

He's angry. Was the kiss my fault?

"I'm okay." Even though the words may not have been true, she kept her voice firm. How could she be okay after a wild kiss like that?

"I want to make sure. Come on, let's go." He slipped his hand under her elbow, but otherwise kept his distance as they headed toward the house.

When they were inside, he guided her to lie on the living room sofa then put a cushion under her head and covered her with the blanket. "Don't want you to get chilled. With the air conditioning, there's quite a temperature change between indoors and outside."

As he bent over her to adjust the cover, Sara kept her gaze averted, focusing on the fireplace across the room. Eye contact at close quarters had led to the kiss. She didn't want to risk that again.

She needed to be alone. She wanted to tell him to stop fussing over her, to just leave. However, she sensed he too was upset and yet had put her well-being ahead of his own discomfort.

Jackson finished tucking the blanket around her. "Want some tea or water or anything?"

"No, thanks." Just go.

"I'll get you some water, in case you want some later."

After bringing a glass of water and placing it on the coffee table within easy reach, he finally left.

She waited until she heard the back door open and close, and then exhaled a deep breath of relief. And let in the memories. Her mind reeled. He had kissed her, and she had kissed him back. She'd wound her arms around him and drawn him close. Being so long in the hot sun must have made her lose her head.

Yeah, right. Blame her behavior on the sun.

After awhile, Sara's strength returned. She sat up, reached for the glass of water and took a long drink. Mentally, she thanked Jackson for his thoughtfulness. She put down the glass, slowly eased to her feet, and took a few tentative steps forward. Her legs were steady.

Physically, she felt fine.

Emotionally, she was a mess.

She'd enjoyed kissing Jackson. In fact, she'd loved every wonderful moment. Being in his arms had been heaven on earth.

As many times as she'd kissed Grayson, she'd always been left cold, where only one kiss from Jackson had set her on fire. She didn't want to fall in love with him. She was here only temporarily. Moreover, she'd lied about her loss of memory. If he learned of her deception, he'd be furious. Maybe he'd even throw her out.

Perhaps she should leave before that happened. Yet, with no money, where would she go? Was staying here, at least until her head injury healed, her only option?

She sighed. Brooding frustrated her. If she were home on Long Island, she'd head for the kitchen and cook something. Cooking was her pathway to peace of mind.

Why not do the same thing here? At home, she'd have to work around Sophie. Although accommodating and cooperative, the Carleton's cook and housekeeper still considered the kitchen her territory.

Here, with Anna Gabraldi away and Jackson out working, there was no one to worry about. Sara strode into the kitchen then stopped, hands on her hips, and looked around. There must be something she could whip up, even with Jackson's limited supplies.

****

In the stable, Jackson gave Lady Mary a vigorous swipe with the brush. The horse jumped sideways. "Sorry, girl. Shouldn't take out my frustration on you."

Yet, he had a pile of emotions he needed to work off. Probably more anger than frustration. Anger for the stupid thing he'd done. Anger at Sara for being so desirable that in a weak moment he'd lost control and kissed her. Anger at Rose for insisting they help Sara in the first place.

Blame bounced around in Jackson's head like a bronco just let out of the chute - and kept coming squarely back to him. The kiss was his fault. He'd promised Sara she didn't need to worry about anything happening, and look what he'd done.

She was every bit as kissable as he'd imagined. Her lips were warm and soft and tender. He'd loved her honey-sweet taste, the silkiness of her hair against his cheek, the softness of her breasts against his chest.

He wasn't exactly starved for a woman's kisses, either. Just a couple of weeks ago, goaded by Rose, he'd taken Trisha Morgan to a dance in Red Rock. At the end of the evening, when she'd leaned close and looked up with big brown eyes, he'd kissed her.

When Trisha's kiss had left him unmoved, he'd told himself he just wasn't ready for a new relationship. But today, kissing Sara had felt like a match thrown on fresh tinder.

Okay, so he felt a physical attraction for her that he didn't feel for Trisha. He still wasn't ready for anything serious.

Why not have a brief affair with Sara? When the time came for her to leave, they would say good-bye and take away memories of good fun and no harm done.

The passion she'd put into their kiss left no doubt she wanted him. She'd put her arms around him and pressed her body close. He'd felt her heart racing, her hot breath like fire against his skin.

From the first glance in the crowded train station, they had been attracted to each other. An attraction apparently unaffected by her loss of memory. Why fight it? What would be the harm? Giving in to their feelings would certainly ease the tension.

His fingers tightened on the brush. How could he even think about taking advantage of Sara while she was vulnerable? Besides, she might already have a husband or a boyfriend. He couldn't risk getting involved when her unknown past hovered over them like a dark cloud. No way. He was nuts to even consider such a wild idea.

Just plain nuts.

Jackson finished brushing Lady Mary, gave her a final pat on the rump, and left her in her stall. He took his time putting away the tack. He straightened the row of bridles hanging from their hooks, and even swept out the room, a job usually reserved for the ranch hands.

Finally, when he could delay no longer, he headed for the house. The back door stood open and a pleasant aroma wafted from the kitchen. He lifted his nose and sniffed the air.

Freshly baked cookies?

His mouth watered, his nose twitched. He opened the door and entered the kitchen.

Sure enough, Sara was removing a tray of cookies from the oven.

"What's going on?" he asked, then realized he had asked an obvious question.

She glanced over her shoulder. "I'm making cookies. Hope you don't mind."

"I don't. But you sure made a speedy recovery."

"I felt better and wanted to cook something. It always—" Picking up a spatula, she twisted it in her hands. "I mean, cooking was just something I wanted to do." She began scooping the cookies onto a wire oven rack on the counter.

Remembering the messy accident with the pot of chicken sauce, he approached her cautiously. "Mind if I try one?"

"Help yourself."

Jackson grabbed a cookie as it slid onto the rack. He tossed it from hand to hand for a couple of seconds while it cooled. Then he took a bite. Warm and chewy, it melted in his mouth. He finished the cookie in a couple more bites. "What kind is this?"

She shrugged. "I don't know. I made up the recipe from what I found in the cupboard."

"Hmmm. I taste coconut."

"Yes."

"And chocolate."

"Uh huh."

Unable to resist, he reached for another one. "These are great, but are you sure you feel okay?"

"I'm sure. I wish you'd quit asking me." Sara picked up a mixing bowl and spooned more globs of cookie dough onto the sheet. She pressed each one into a flat circle.

He studied her. Maybe she felt well enough to be cooking, but something bothered her. Even though he'd known her only a few days, her refusal to meet his gaze indicated all was not well. Their kiss must've upset her, too. He wanted to apologize, reassure her there'd be no more kissing. "Sara, about what happened out there awhile ago—"

She interrupted him. "We don't need to talk about it, Jackson."

"We do need to talk."

He'd learned all about good communication from Cathleen. She'd always shared her feelings and had encouraged him to do so as well. At first, talking about his emotions made him uncomfortable. He'd always patterned himself after his dad, an aloof individual who'd kept things to himself.

But, with Cathleen's gentle and patient guidance, he'd learned to open up and share what was on his mind. He tried again. "I've learned talking helps."

"Not in this case, because I've made a decision, and discussing what happened is unnecessary."

How could someone without her memory make a decision? His jaw dropped. "A decision?"

"Yes, I intended to wait until after dinner to tell you, but now seems as good a time as any." She turned to face him, squared her shoulders, and lifted her chin. "Jackson, I—"

The wall phone rang. They both jumped.

"Hang on a minute," he told Sara, then leaped to the phone and snatched up the receiver.

"Rolling R ranch. Jackson speaking."

Chapter Six

While Jackson talked on the phone, Sara
cleaned the kitchen. She wished the call hadn't
interrupted them. She'd been about to tell him that,
although she appreciated his generosity, she couldn't
stay there any longer. She'd ask for a small loan,
and that he take her into town where she could get a
room. Then she'd look for a job. Surely, there was
something she could do. Maybe a position with
training provided. She'd take anything within
reason to earn some money.

Deep in thought, she hadn't paid much attention
to Jackson's end of the phone conversation. She
glanced his way and was surprised to meet his direct
gaze.

"No, her memory hasn't returned yet," he said.
"Oh? No kidding?"

The phone call was about her? Sara's heart
raced.

"Is that right?" Jackson said. "I see."

She wished he'd say something to indicate who
the caller was and exactly what they were talking
about. And why hadn't the person asked to speak to
her personally?

The conversation went on, with Jackson making
only noncommittal remarks. She wanted to yank the
phone from his hand and speak to the caller herself.
They were talking about her future. Instead, she
picked up the dishcloth and swiped at the counter.

"Okay," he said. "Tomorrow at ten a.m. Yeah,
we'll be there." He hung up.

"Where will we be?" Fear hardened her voice.

"Who was that?"

Jackson held up his hand. "Whoa, one thing at a time. That was Sergeant Roger Decker of the Red Rock Police. The photo of you they sent out—"

She gasped. "Someone recognized me?"

"Yes, someone did."

"Oh, my." Sara pressed both hands to her cheeks. Her skin burned underneath her fingers.

"The guy is flying to Denver tomorrow. Decker wants us at the Red Rock Station when he arrives."

"Flying in from where?" Sara could barely manage to speak.

"I don't know. Back east someplace."

Back east? Long Island, New York? "What's the man's name?"

"I didn't ask."

"You didn't find out much, did you?"

Jackson picked up the phone receiver and thrust it at her. "Here, why don't you call Decker and talk to him yourself?"

Her heart thudding, Sara reached for the receiver. Then she dropped her arm. "Never mind. I'm sorry. This has been so upsetting—"

Jackson replaced the receiver. He took a step toward her then stopped. "I know," he said. "It's been hard on me, too. But aren't you glad that tomorrow you might find out who you are?"

"I, yes, I guess so. You'll be glad if I do, won't you?" She cast him a sideways look.

"What? Me?" He cleared his throat then said, "Well, sure. The sooner you get your problem solved, the better. But, hey, you were about to tell me something before the phone call interrupted us."

She waved a hand. "Oh, never mind. It wasn't anything important."

That night, Sara laid awake wondering whom she would face at the Red Rock Police Station. She doubted her father would come and claim her. He'd probably sent Grayson. If not Grayson, one of his employees.

No matter who came, what would she do? Continue her loss of memory charade? Or come clean and admit she knew her identity?

When morning came, and she and Jackson were on their way to Red Rock, Sara stared out the pickup's window at the passing countryside. The sun cast a golden light over the purple hills and distant mountain peaks. Wispy clouds chased each other across a turquoise sky, while a light breeze swept tumbleweeds across the flat, brown land.

Although she'd been in Colorado only a few days, she'd come to appreciate the open spaces. They gave her a sense of freedom. Freedom to do as she pleased, go where she pleased.

Now, as she and Jackson headed to Red Rock to meet Grayson, or whomever her father had sent, her freedom was about to be snatched away.

The situation was not fair. She sighed and smoothed the front of her gray jacket. Along with her navy blue slacks, this was the outfit she'd worn the day she'd arrived in Red Rock. Jackson had sent the clothes to the cleaners and they were all fresh and nicely pressed. She had a new purse, too, a bright red one, that Molly gave her.

"There's a penny in it," Molly had told her when she'd brought the purse to Jackson's house. "For good luck."

She could use some of that. "I appreciate your taking me into town," she said, breaking what had become an uncomfortable silence. "I know how busy you are."

He shot her a glance. "You couldn't drive yourself, now, could you?"

His sarcasm jolted her. What was going on? He should be happy to be rid of her. "No, but one of your ranch hands could've given me a lift."

"You don't like my company?"

Sara folded her arms across her chest. "Your company is fine."

Was he trying to pick a fight? She didn't want to fight. If anything, she wanted peace between them. This would be the last time they were together.

His gaze glued to the road, Jackson fell silent. After a few moments, she glanced at him and let her gaze trace his high forehead, bold nose, and firm chin with just a hint of beard. Her heart skipped a beat. He certainly was handsome.

Her attention focused on his arms. His denim shirt was rolled up to the elbows, as usual, exposing muscular forearms. She remembered the breathless thrill of being in those arms. Of looking into his dark eyes. Of kissing him.

Yes, those moments had been wonderful - and all too brief.

But the kiss had been a mistake. The kiss had spoiled their budding camaraderie and friendship. Since then, she'd felt awkward and self-conscious around him.

Well, after today, she wouldn't have to worry how she felt in his presence. She wouldn't have to worry about him at all. Sara shifted in her seat and looked out the window again, wishing that, even if she had to face her father soon, this trip were over with.

Half an hour later, Sara's heart hammered as she and Jackson entered the yellow brick police station. What would happen inside? Would Grayson make an ugly scene when he saw her? Or would he just quietly whisk her away and back to Long Island?

Inside the station, a man with a salt-and-pepper crew cut and wearing navy slacks and a light blue shirt stepped from behind a counter. "Hey, Jackson," he said, then turned to Sara and extended his hand.

"I'm Roger Decker. Remember me? I came to the hospital after you were brought in."

Sara accepted his handshake. "Uh, no, I'm sorry, I don't remember you." She looked to Jackson for confirmation and was relieved when he nodded.

"So where's the guy?" Jackson asked.

"He's not here yet," Roger said.

Sara's heart swelled with hope. Perhaps he wasn't coming. Perhaps her father had changed his mind and decided not to make her return home, after all.

Roger turned back to Sara. "Don't look so scared, little lady. He called and said his plane was late."

"I can't help but be nervous." She wished the policeman had mentioned a name.

He gave her a fatherly pat on the shoulder. "C'mon, I have a room where you can wait."

Roger led them through the station's main room toward a hallway. A woman and a man sitting behind their respective desks looked up, eyebrows raised in curiosity.

They'd undoubtedly heard all about the stranger with amnesia. Sara managed to send them a smile. The woman waved and the man offered a solemn nod. As she continued down the hall, she felt their gazes bore into her back.

The room where Roger delivered them had a rectangular table and several straight chairs upholstered in dull beige vinyl. A bulletin board on the wall held a haphazard arrangement of notices. The only windows were in the door and the wall facing the hall.

Sara ground to a halt in the doorway, the hair on her arms rising. *This is where they grill suspects. I don't want to go in there.*

"Sara?"

Roger's voice prodded her to action. "Uh, yes, okay." She crossed the threshold and perched on the edge of one of the chairs. The room had a musty smell, as though it hadn't been aired out for a while.

"I have errands to do," Jackson said. "I'll be back later."

She twisted around to look at him, then quickly away, lest he see her fear. *Don't leave me here!* She wanted to run to him and beg to be taken along. But then he might think she didn't want to find out the so-called truth about herself. Biting back the words, she nodded instead.

Through the window, she watched Roger and Jackson while they stood in the hallway talking. Then Jackson left. Emptiness crept into her heart.

Roger opened the door and peeked in. "You okay? Want coffee or anything?"

I want out of here. "I'm fine, thank you."

Someone called, "Roger, phone!"

"Oh oh, gotta go." He shut the door.

And Sara was alone. She kept her back rigid, trying not to worry or track the passing minutes on the wall clock. She wished now she'd asked for coffee. Even if she didn't drink it, holding the cup would give her hands something to do.

Time crept by. Sara finally rose and paced around the table. She looked at the bulletin board notices - a city council meeting, the policemen's guild election, the upcoming county fair.

At last, footsteps sounded in the hallway. Someone was coming. She held her breath and waited for the door to open.

"Sara?"

She turned and faced the door.

Roger, his hand on the doorknob, stood aside while another man entered the room.

She started. He wasn't Grayson, as she'd expected, but someone she'd never seen before. One of her father's men? He didn't look like the kind her father hired. They tended to be husky and sharp-eyed, while the man who stood before her was small-built, and his eyes had a vacant look.

"Do you want me to stay?" Roger asked.

Sara debated. Although she didn't particularly want to be alone with the stranger, if he had been sent by her father, she'd better talk to him without a police witness. "I'll be okay," she told Roger.

"I'll be close by, if you need me," he said.

Roger had barely closed the door before the man scurried to her side. "So, I've found you!" he exclaimed.

Sara opened her mouth to say something about her father.

"Martha, you can't imagine how worried I've been about you. Come here and let me kiss you." He opened his arms.

Sara jumped back and held up her hands. "I'm not Martha!"

"Of course, you are." He gave her a crooked grin and shuffled closer. "Oh, they told me you think your name is Sara, but that's because you lost your memory. You're my wife, Martha Howard."

By now, she realized he had nothing to do with her father. Still, she wasn't out of danger. "No, no, I'm not your wife. Don't come any closer, or, I swear, I'll scream." When he stopped his advance, she breathed a sigh of relief.

"Come on, Martha," he wheedled. "You remember. We live in Kansas City. We have two children, Bobby and Betty. You caught the train to visit your mother out in Oregon. But you never arrived and you never came back."

"No, I don't remember that at all."

"Looky here." He whipped a wallet from his back pocket, pulled out a snapshot and held it out. "Now you tell me if that ain't you."

Remaining where she was and crossing her arms over her chest, Sara leaned to look at the photo. A couple with two small children, a boy and a girl, stood in front of a large, white frame house. Although the picture was out of focus, and the woman appeared a few years older than she, Sara had to admit there was a resemblance. "That's not me."

The man's thin mouth turned down.

Thinking he was going to yell, her gaze darted to the closed door. Should she call Roger?

Then his frown turned into a smile. "That's okay, Martha. You'll remember soon as we get home."

Her stomach clenched. "I'm not going anywhere with you."

"Sure you are." He crossed to the door, opened it, and stuck his head out. "Officer!"

Some of her tension seeped away. As soon as Roger arrived, everything would be all right.

Instead of Roger, the man she'd seen sitting at a desk appeared. His nametag said, "Carl Doughty." He crossed the room to where she and Mr. Howard stood.

Before Mr. Howard could speak, Sara blurted, "I'm not this man's wife."

Mr. Howard's head bobbed. "Sure, you bet she is."

Carl scratched his bald head and looked at Sara. "If you have amnesia, how do you know you aren't his wife?"

"Because..." How could she convince Carl without giving herself away?

"Looky here at this picture." Mr. Howard thrust the photo at the officer.

Carl studied the picture then focused on Sara. "Sure looks like you're right on, Mr. Howard."

Sara's palms began to sweat. "Where's Roger?"

"He had to step out for a minute," Carl said.

"We don't need to wait for him." Mr. Howard

held out his hand to Sara. "Come on, Martha, I'll take you home."

She stepped away from him. "I'm not going anywhere until Roger returns," she told the officer. "And Jackson, too. He should be back any time now."

Carl frowned. "Why do you have to wait for them? I can handle this."

"Because...because I have something to tell them."

Carl blew out a breath and scratched his head again. "Boy, this is some dilemma."

Just then, Roger arrived. He stood in the doorway, hands propped on his hips, and scanned the group. "What's going on?"

Carl explained what had transpired while he was gone.

Roger looked at Sara. "Officer Doughty has a point, little lady. How do you know you're not Howard's wife, if you have amnesia?"

Sara's eyes burned with tears. "I, I just know, that's all. Please, this is very upsetting." She sank into a chair and put her face in her hands. Any minute now, she would have to blurt out the truth.

Roger narrowed his gaze at Mr. Howard. "Do you have any other proof, besides this photo?"

Howard took a step toward the door. "I, uh, gotta go to the men's room."

"Okay, it's down the hall. We'll wait."

After Mr. Howard left, the woman officer stuck her head in the door. "Important fax for you," she said to Roger.

Roger hurried from the room. Sara and Officer Doughty waited in silence. Sara's stomach twisted into a painful knot. She wanted this awful scene over with. She expected Mr. Howard to return from the men's room any moment.

Roger appeared first, waving a sheet of paper. "Where's Howard?"

"He ain't come back yet," Carl said.

"Go find him!"

Carl Doughty hurried from the room, almost colliding with Jackson.

Sara's heart took a leap. Thank God, Jackson was back. She wanted to cheer and run into his arms, but forced herself to remain still. The matter of Mr. Howard wasn't solved yet.

"How'd it go?" Jackson asked, his gaze swinging from Roger to Sara. "Something's wrong. What?"

"You bet your bippy something's wrong." Roger waved the paper. "Howard's a nut case. We just got a fax from the Kansas City police. His sister notified them he was on his way here."

Jackson's eyebrows shot up. "What did he do to you, Sara? He didn't hurt you, did he?"

His concern brought the tears back to her eyes. "No, he didn't hurt me. He scared me, though, the way he kept calling me Martha and insisting I'm his wife."

"And you're not?" Jackson asked.

"No way!"

"But, how do you know—" Jackson began.

"According to the sister," Roger interrupted, "Howard's wife did leave him a couple of years ago. She got on a train and never came back. For some reason, which no one quite understands, he believed the reason she didn't come back was because she had amnesia. Every time an amnesiac woman turns up, he tries to claim her. Medication has helped the problem, but he recently stopped taking it."

"Whew! That's quite a story," Jackson said.

Carl poked his head in the room. "Can't find him anywhere."

"Keep looking!" Roger said.

"Okay," Carl said, "but she said she has something to tell you both." He pointed a finger at Sara.

Both men swiveled to look at her.

"What?" Jackson said.

Sara stared at the floor. "I, uh, nothing, really. I was just stalling for time. You know."

Jackson came over and put his arm around her waist. "That was good thinking, Sara. It must've been a terrible ordeal."

Warmed and comforted by his gesture, she rested her head on his shoulder.

Jackson turned to Roger. "Can I take her home now?"

Home. Sara hadn't thought of Jackson's ranch as "home," but, right now, there was no place she'd rather be.

"I don't see why not," Roger said. "I'm sure sorry, little lady, to put you through all this. If only I had known..."

"It's all right," Sara said, relieved that her "ordeal," as Jackson had called it, was finally over.

Jackson said, "We're not holding you responsible, Roger. I feel sorry for the guy. If you find him, try to help him, okay?"

"Will do," Roger said. "And we'll hope the next person who comes for Sara is the real thing."

Chapter Seven

Outside the station, Jackson studied Sara. Her shoulders slumped and shaking hands clutched the purse Molly had given her. He berated himself for abandoning her earlier. But he hadn't wanted to witness her reunion with the man who was probably her husband or boyfriend.

"I'm sorry you had to go through that," he said. "But we didn't know, did we?"

"Right. Who would have guessed?" She gave him a faint smile.

"You might feel better if you ate something. Lunchtime." He pointed to his wristwatch.

She nodded. "I could eat a little."

"I know a good short order place."

He guided them around the corner to The Roundup Restaurant.

As they entered, the middle-aged hostess stepped forward. "Back so soon?"

"Yes, Agnes, this time, for lunch." He turned to Sara. "I had a cup of coffee here after I ran my errand." He'd gone to Lowe's Feed Store, then spent the rest of the time sitting at The Roundup's counter, worrying about Sara and the man who'd come to claim her.

Agnes led them to a corner booth. When the waitress had taken their orders and they were alone again, he leaned forward and asked, "You want to talk about it?"

She shrugged. "There's not much to say. He just kept telling me I was his wife, Martha, and he would take me home. Strange thing is, he had a snapshot of him and his family, and his wife did resemble me."

"His sister said he goes after amnesiacs who look like her. Anyway, like I told Roger, his is a sad situation. I hope the guy gets help."

"I do, too."

He let a beat of silence pass and then brought up something that had been weighing on his mind. "You must be disappointed. I mean, of course, you were looking forward to seeing, ah, the person who's missing you."

Sara looked away. "I suppose I feel let down, but relieved, too, that I didn't have to go with Mr. Howard."

"Funny you were so sure he isn't your husband. Does that mean you've remembered something?"

"I, ah, guess my instincts came to my rescue."

He was about to pursue the subject when the waitress came by and refilled their coffee cups.

Sara sat back and looked around. "This is a cute place."

He glanced at the tables covered with checkered cloths and the walls decorated with sepia-toned photos of the Old West. "Yeah, I guess you could say so. I come here so often I don't pay any attention to the décor anymore."

They both fell silent. He stared blankly at the wall photos while she straightened her place setting.

Finally, she said, "Jackson, before Roger Decker called last night, about someone flying in to claim me, I intended to tell you...that I..." She faltered, swallowed, then continued in a rush, "I don't think I should stay at your ranch any longer."

Somehow, her announcement didn't surprise him. "Because of what happened after our horseback ride." He made the words a statement, rather than a question.

She nodded. "Please don't take it personally. But I just can't risk getting involved under these circumstances. A relationship wouldn't be fair to either of us. You understand, don't you?"

"I do."

"Besides, you don't want to get involved with anyone, either."

He gave a start. "How did you know that?"

"Rose told me about your fiancée who passed away. I'm sorry."

The old grief twisted his gut. He took a swallow of coffee, hoping to chase it away. "Yeah, I'm still not used to her being gone. Don't know if I ever will be."

He wasn't angry with Rose for telling Sara about Cathleen. Now she'd know he was unavailable, too.

Sara sipped her water. "I'd like to move into town and get a job somewhere."

"Then what?"

"Just wait and see what happens, I guess."

"But you don't have any money."

She lowered her eyelids. "I thought you might be willing to loan me some. Until I get on my feet, of course. Then I'll pay you back."

"I could do that."

"I'd really appreciate it." Offering him a smile, she leaned back against the booth and exhaled a deep breath.

"I could," he repeated, "but I have a better idea."

Her eyes became wary. "What?"

"You can work for me. And Rose," he added, thinking the inclusion of his sister might make his offer more acceptable. "Take Anna Gabraldi's place. You enjoy cooking. I enjoy eating."

He could hardly believe what he was saying. Yet, this was the plan he'd worked out earlier, on the off chance Sara wouldn't belong to the person she was meeting. Something told him his proposal was more dangerous than riding the wildest bronc in the rodeo, but for some reason, he just couldn't let her go.

Not yet.

"Won't Anna be back soon?" Sara asked.

He shrugged. "Don't know. I'm sure she wouldn't begrudge me hiring a substitute. She tried to find one herself."

"And I'd still stay at your place?"

"It would be more convenient."

She shook her head. "I don't think so."

"If you live somewhere else, how will you get to and from the ranch?"

"You've got a point. But what about...?"

She didn't have to finish the sentence for him to know what she meant. He sucked in a breath. "Now that we both understand neither of us can get involved, I'm confident our staying together won't be a problem."

Her brows furrowed, but she said nothing.

"Besides," he continued, "if you move into town, everyone will wonder why. Rose will be upset. I'll feel like a jerk. Staying at the house would be better - under our new arrangement, of course."

"Hmmm." A soft smile tilted her lips. Then the smile vanished and she said, in a flat voice, "I don't think so."

His spirits dropped like a lead ball. Still, she hadn't said a definite no.

The waitress arrived with their meals. They waited in silence while she set the plates on the table. The aroma of his hamburger drifted up to Jackson's nose, but their unresolved conversation had dulled his appetite.

"Tell you what," he told Sara. "Let's eat, and then you can decide."

****

The first bite of chicken salad stuck in Sara's throat, but when she realized how hungry she really was, the second went down smoothly. She must eat to keep up her strength. Still, the emotional roller coaster she'd been on had set her nerves on edge. She'd been keyed up since last night and again this morning, when she'd thought she would have to confess. Then, when Mr. Howard was exposed and no longer a threat, she relaxed. Not a lot, but at least, a little.

Now, whether or not to accept Jackson's offer posed a new dilemma.

Staying at the Rolling R would be easier than relocating. Accepting the job as his cook, instead of having to hunt for another position, would be easier, too. Finding another job might take awhile. She had no idea of Red Rock's employment opportunities.

What about their attraction to each other? They had given in and kissed.

But that was all they'd done. And now, after their little talk, they understood neither one wanted to become involved. What was there to worry about? From here on, they had an understanding. From here on, she would be his employee, nothing more.

Sara finished her last bite of chicken salad and laid her fork across her empty plate.

Jackson put down his fork at the same time. "More coffee? Dessert? Anything?"

"No, thanks. I'm fine."

Keeping one eye on her, he reached for the check. "What'll it be, then? Back to the ranch or to a hotel?"

Sara bit her lower lip, and then said, softly, "Back to the Rolling R."

****

On the way to his truck, Jackson noticed Sara's mood had improved. She stood taller and had a smile on her lips. She gazed at shop windows with interest and curiosity.

When they came to a clothing store, she stopped in front of the window display. "That's pretty." She pointed to a mannequin wearing a flared, blue skirt and a matching knit top.

The vision of Sara dressed in the outfit popped into Jackson's mind. The blue was the same shade as her eyes. The soft knit top clung to her breasts and the skirt molded to her rounded hips. The skirt also revealed legs he hadn't fully seen, but, judging from her slim ankles, were long and shapely. His temperature shot up a couple degrees.

"That would look great on you," he said. "Which reminds me, you need some new clothes."

"I know." She wrinkled her brow.

"Feel up to picking out some right now? Might as well, since we're here."

"Maybe I should wait until I get my first paycheck."

"How 'bout I give you an advance on your salary?"

She tipped her head, and then smiled. "It would be nice to have a few things of my own."

"Then come on, let's do it." Grabbing her hand, he led her into the store.

A few minutes later, Jackson sat near the fitting rooms watching Sara search through the racks of clothing. Not wanting to interfere and not knowing anything about women's clothing—except how it looked on the woman—he had retreated to the sidelines.

Sara kept the sales clerk busy carting outfits into the dressing room. Although he couldn't see the price tags when they were whisked by, her choices all looked expensive.

Later, dressed each time in a different outfit, she emerged from the dressing room to give him his own private fashion show.

"What do you think?" she asked, parading by in a fringed skirt and jacket decorated with gold studs and colored beads.

"Looks terrific. They all do, but—"

Her head jerked around. "What?"

"Not very practical for a ranch cook."

The joyous light vanished from her eyes.

Sorry he'd spoiled her fun, he rushed on, "Look, why don't you pick out a couple of these for special occasions...should any come along. Then get yourself some jeans and T-shirts, a plain jacket, a hat, and a pair of boots. That ought to be enough for starters."

"You're right. What was I thinking?"

He waved a hand. "Relax. You were having fun. All women love to shop, don't they? Didn't a woman invent the phrase, 'Shop till you drop'?"

"Probably." She smiled then pressed a hand to her temple. "I'm about to drop right now."

"Hang on a little longer. And remember, you don't have to buy your entire wardrobe today. There'll be plenty of opportunities to come into town later."

Sara selected her two fancy outfits and their more practical counterparts. They moved to another part of the store where Jackson helped her choose a hat and boots.

"There are some other things I need." She pointed to the lingerie department. "Why don't you, um, take a break for a few minutes?"

He raised his eyebrows and grinned. "Sure you don't want my advice in that area, too?"

A rosy blush crept over her cheeks. "No, thanks."

He couldn't help teasing her a little more. "You're passing up an expert's opinion."

"I'm sure I am," she said dryly. "Now, get lost for a couple of minutes."

He did, while his imagination went to work on what she might be choosing. A few minutes later, when she headed toward the cash register, he caught up with her. As the clerk rang up her purchases, he glimpsed lacy items in shades of cream, rose, and blue. No doubt about it, the lady had great taste in clothing.

On the way back to the ranch, Jackson noticed Sara's head begin to nod. Maybe the morning had been too much exertion. "Go ahead and take a nap," he said. "You've had a busy day."

She shot him a grateful smile. "I certainly have...and Jackson—"

"Yeah?"

"Thanks." Her smile widened.

"For the advance on the clothes? Sure. No problem."

"For that, yes. But also for sticking by me today."

After leaving for a trumped-up errand, he wasn't sure he deserved her appreciation. "Even though I abandoned you at first?"

"Yes, even so. You were there later, when I needed help."

"I've gotta ask again, though, are you sorry you're coming home with me?"

She shook her head. "Not so far."

Relief washed over him. "Good. Relax and take a nap."

"Okay, boss."

Sara twisted a shoulder and laid her head against the seat. Soon her even breathing indicated she was asleep. As he rounded a corner, she slid toward him and her head came to rest on his shoulder. She stirred and attempted to right herself.

"It's okay." He reached over and pulled her against him.

"Mmmm," she murmured.

Jackson ached to slip his arm around her and draw her even closer. But, besides being bad for his driving, the gesture didn't fit with their new, hands-off agreement. The pleasant sensation of her head against his shoulder would have to do.

Sara was coming home with him. His chest swelled with an emotion he couldn't name, but one that made him happier than he'd been in ages.

Dark lashes fanned her cheeks, a sharp contrast to her creamy skin. Her soft, pink lips were moist and slightly parted. With a sudden rush of heat he remembered holding her in his arms and kissing those lips.

No, don't go there!

Misgivings haunted Jackson. Was he kidding himself—and Sara—about keeping their mutual attraction under control? Did he want her to remain at the ranch, hoping the tension would get so unbearable they would give in and fall into bed?

He should forget their attraction and concentrate on helping to restore her memory. Who was she, anyway?

Her manicured nails, her expensive taste in clothes, and the graceful way she carried herself suggested she came from a wealthy and cultured background. Even if Mr. Howard hadn't been the one, Jackson was sure that somewhere, someone was missing Sara.

****

J. Edward paced his high-rise Manhattan office while he waited for Grayson to arrive. Should he tell the young man the news about Sara? He really didn't want to, but neither did he know how he could avoid it. Grayson was all for making Sara's absence public knowledge. J. Edward hoped what he told Grayson today would change his mind.

When a week passed with no further word from his runaway daughter, he'd been worried himself. But now he had no doubt what was going on.

The intercom on the phone buzzed. He punched the button. "Yes, Alice?"

"Grayson is here."

"Send him in."

A moment later, Grayson entered. J. Edward cringed when he saw the other man's yellow tie and charcoal gray suit combination. Did he think it was Halloween? He stuffed down his criticism. No need to risk riling the man today. Wait until after Grayson and Sara's marriage to work on the younger man's wardrobe.

Grayson hurried to J. Edward's desk and sank into a chair. "You heard from Sara?"

"In a manner of speaking, yes."

"You didn't actually talk to her? I thought she might have called again."

"This is better than a call." J. Edward picked up several fax sheets lying on his desk and held them out.

Grayson studied the papers. "Where'd you get these?"

"From the credit card company. An employee owes me a favor. The bill eventually would come to the house, but this way, we don't have to wait."

Grayson ran a finger down one of the sheets. "Sara's charged a lot."

J. Edward nodded. "She maxed out the card, which is not surprising. You know how she likes to shop."

"Mostly clothes, I see, but here's a diamond ring. Why does she want another diamond when she has her engagement ring?"

He wasn't going to tell Grayson he'd found the engagement ring in Sara's bedroom. No sense in upsetting him any further. He shrugged. "She likes jewelry."

Grayson frowned and then studied the faxes again. "A leather coat? Sara wouldn't buy that. And here's one for a gold chain. Gold chains are so seventies. No one wears them anymore, except gangsters."

"I admit some of her purchases are unusual."

72

"Are you sure these signatures are hers?" Grayson's fist tightened and the papers rustled. "Are you sure the card wasn't stolen?"

"The handwriting looks authentic to me," J. Edward answered truthfully. "And, wouldn't she report a stolen card? She can't live without her charge cards."

Grayson paced the room, waving the faxes. "Where were these purchases made?"

"In the Denver area."

"What would she be doing in Denver? Does she have friends there?"

"Not that I know of. We've been skiing a few times at Aspen and Vail, though, so she's familiar with the area."

"It's not skiing season now."

"I know that!" J. Edward snapped. "I'm just trying to answer your question."

Grayson wrinkled his forehead. "Sorry, but I'm worried about her."

"You think I'm not?" J. Edward tapped his fingers on his desktop.

"Of course, you are. You're her father. But I feel we should do something more than just wait."

"I'm as stubborn as she is. I can wait until she gives up and comes home."

Grayson leveled his gaze at J. Edward. "You really think she made these purchases, then?"

"Yes, I do. She's angry with me and not thinking clearly."

"How many more credit cards does she have?"

"Several," J. Edward admitted.

"Well, then, we may have a long wait."

****

Back in his own office, away from J. Edward's domineering presence and authority, Grayson knew he wasn't going to wait. He had already contacted a private detective, who hadn't turned up anything.

But now there was more to check out. He looked up the man's number, and then reached for the phone to give him the news about Denver.

Chapter Eight

Sara pulled the cookie sheet from the oven and scooped the freshly baked cookies onto the wire rack. Each time she made a batch, she experimented with the recipe. This version included dried cherries and walnuts.

Today, she'd take the cookies to the ranch bunkhouse. Molly tired easily, and Sara had volunteered to help cook for the ranch hands. After several visits, she and Molly were becoming good friends.

As Sara cleaned up the kitchen, she thought about the past two weeks. The memory of the awful meeting with Mr. Howard still lingered. Roger Decker told them Howard's sister arrived to escort him back to Kansas City. She promised to make sure he took his meds and would consult the doctor to see if anything more could be done for him.

Even though the unfortunate ordeal turned out all right, Sara knew she wasn't safe from her father. If they thought to check on people reported as amnesiacs, he and Grayson could still find her. Or, they could report her missing and alert authorities all over the country. She doubted her father would resort to the latter, though. He hated scandal and guarded his personal life from public scrutiny. Thank goodness, she'd phoned him from the train station. Otherwise, he might have assumed the worst and already filed a missing person's report.

Whenever the phone rang, she held her breath, thinking Roger Decker might be summoning her to the police station to meet someone. So far, though, no one besides poor Mr. Howard had looked her up.

Taking advantage of the situation, even though temporary, Sara immersed herself in her new role as Jackson's cook. The kitchen became her domain. She knew where every pan, every dish was kept. She knew the contents of the spice cupboard and the freezer. Every minute she spent there gave her pleasure.

On the down side were Anna's housekeeping duties, which weren't as easy as the cooking. Anna's bottles and cans of cleaner bewildered Sara, who never did any cleaning at home. However, reading the labels and experimenting had helped.

She wished her relationship with Jackson were doing as well as her job. Mornings weren't so bad, because he was in a hurry to get to work. Most days, he was up and out of the house before she came downstairs. The evenings, however, were long and tension-filled. Not even the television could make her forget he was nearby, and sometimes she'd glance up and catch him staring.

He'd clear his throat and glance away. Or, he'd jump up and mumble something about having work to do in his office.

Then she'd sit alone until time to go to bed. Often, she'd lie awake until his footsteps sounded on the stairs, then hold her breath until he passed by her room.

She'd had a couple of dreams of being in his arms again, and one in which Grayson and her father hovered in the background, shouting at her. After the last one, she'd woken up in a sweat and had lain awake a long time before falling back to sleep.

Sara placed the last dirty dish in the dishwasher and wiped the counter clean. She touched a fingertip to one of the cookies and decided they were cool enough to put in a plastic container to take to the bunkhouse.

Before leaving, she went into the bathroom to freshen up. She picked up her comb and, looking in the mirror, ran it through her hair. Her gaze lighted on the spot where she'd had the head injury. Last week, Jackson had taken her into Red Rock to see Dr. Mike Mahoney. He'd removed the stitches, checked her over, and pronounced her as good as new.

The hair trimmed away from the wound was growing back. She'd be glad when it was long enough to keep her head from looking lop-sided.

She put down her comb and smoothed her T-shirt over the waistband of her jeans. Her new clothes pleased her. She'd lost her head on the shopping excursion with Jackson, though, and picked out expensive items, forgetting she was supposed to be a penniless amnesiac in Red Rock, Colorado, instead of a wealthy Long Island heiress. Good thing Jackson hadn't questioned her about her penchant for nice clothes.

Still, guilt nagged her. She was living a lie that might come crashing down at any time. Then what would happen? The truth would destroy all the good will she'd built up with Jackson and Rose, and her other new friends on the ranch. She'd return to her old life and the same dilemma she'd had before.

Determined not to worry, Sara straightened her shoulders and lifted her chin. She'd begun the day full of enthusiasm for making the cookies and helping Molly with lunch. She should be at the bunkhouse right now. Hurrying back to the kitchen, she picked up the tub of cookies and went out the door.

At the bunkhouse, Sara handed the cookies to Molly.

The other woman opened the container and looked inside. "Oh, these look wonderful. The guys are gonna love 'em."

Sara beamed at Molly's approval of her offering and then gazed around the kitchen. The large, square room had plenty of cupboards, stainless steel counters, two double sinks, and a butcher's block in the center. "What can I do to help?"

Molly gestured to a counter where a loaf of bread sat on a breadboard. "How 'bout making the sandwiches? There's sliced beef and cheese in the fridge. I'll tend to the soup." One hand on her stomach, she waddled to the stove. "Ouch, the baby just kicked me."

Sara crossed the room to the counter. "He's eager to enter the world. The wait's almost over, isn't it?"

"Just a few more weeks, if I'm on time. And I sure hope I am."

"How many sandwiches should I make?"

"A couple each for the guys, one for me, and whatever you want for yourself."

Sara picked up a knife and sliced into the homemade bread. A rich, yeasty aroma wafted to her nose and stirred hunger pangs in her stomach.

"Any signs of your memory returning yet?" Molly asked.

"Memory is a funny thing," Sara said, keeping her voice pitched low.

"My friend Cassie told me about a woman hypnotist in Red Rock. She was on TV awhile back and said she helps people recover lost memories. Cassie thought maybe hypnosis would help her lose weight, so she made an appointment. Afterward, Cassie told the hypnotist about you, and she said she could help you. I gave her card to Jackson."

The knife slipped from Sara's fingers and clattered onto the board. "Oh, no!"

Molly stopped stirring the soup and frowned. "Why not? Your memory hasn't returned on its own."

"I know, but, uh-" Sara groped for a reason to stay far away from the hypnotist. "Hypnosis has always scared me."

Molly narrowed her eyes. "How do you know that if you can't remember your past?"

Ouch. She'd done it again. Always some pitfall to stumble into. "What I meant was, seeing a hypnotist scares me right now, probably because of that awful experience with Mr. Howard."

"Well, if it was me, I'd try any means I could to get my life back."

"I am. I mean, I will. But I want to be the one to contact her, okay?"

"Hey, I was just trying to help. I guess I should learn to mind my own business." Molly turned back to the stove and stirred the soup.

"Oh, Molly, I'm sorry. Please don't be upset with me. I appreciate your help. I really do. I'll talk it over with Jackson. Okay?"

"Whatever," Molly mumbled.

Sara knew Molly was still upset. She regretted offending her new friend, but no way did she want to see the hypnotist. She feared the woman would know she was faking her memory loss.

The clop-clop of horses approaching drifted in the open window. The men were coming, a welcome interruption to the tension between Sara and Molly.

"They're here," Sara said. "I'd better hurry with these sandwiches."

A few minutes later, while Sara stacked the sandwiches on a plate, the men entered the dining room. Their feet thumped on the wooden floor and their voices rose and fell as they crossed the room and settled themselves at the table. She peeked through the doorway and saw Sandy, Phil, and Diego.

Phil, a lean man in his late thirties, pulled a checkered handkerchief from a jeans pocket and wiped his high forehead. "Just don't get too involved with your gal friend, Diego, or you'll end up like me. Twice divorced and took to the cleaners ever' time."

Sandy scratched his white beard. At fifty, he was the oldest of the crew. "Aw, let him find out for hisself."

"What do you know about it?" Phil challenged. "You ain't never been married."

"No, but that hasn't kept me away from the women. I reckon I got more experience with 'em than you."

"Maria, she wants to get married." Diego spoke in his softly accented voice.

"You mean her papa wants her to get married," Phil scoffed. "I seen the way he hovers over her when they come into town."

"Yeah," Sandy chimed in, "he wants to make sure you're hog tied and tamed before there's one in the oven."

Sandy and Phil both laughed, but at Diego's glower, they let their laughter fade away.

"Wonder if Jackson will ever tie the knot?" Phil said.

"Don't know." Sandy said. "He was awful broke up when his gal passed away."

"He still is," Diego put in.

"This new gal's awful pretty, though," Phil said. "Nice, too. And I seen the way he looks at her. Like one of them new calves we got."

The men laughed then Sandy put a finger to his lips. "We better shut up. Here comes Jackson and Buck. And she's probably in the kitchen fixin' our lunch."

Sara's cheeks flamed. She glanced at Molly and saw she too had overheard the conversation.

"Don't pay them any mind," Molly said. "They don't mean any harm. It's just guy talk."

Yet, when Sara brought in the sandwiches, and

Jackson made a special point of greeting her, the others stared openly. Surely, his attention didn't mean anything; he was just being friendly.

Yeah, right. No denying it, something more than friendship was developing between them. The big question was, what were they going to do about it?

At the end of the meal, Molly brought in Sara's cookies, holding the plate aloft, as though it were a prize. "Da da! Here's a treat from our excellent cook, Sara!"

Relieved her friend had apparently put aside her hurt over their earlier discussion about the hypnotist, Sara watched the plate pass from hand to hand, with each man taking several.

"These are really tasty," Phil said around a mouthful.

"Sara made up the recipe herself," Jackson said.

"No kiddin'?" Buck said.

Sandy pointed a gnarly finger at Sara. "You ought to enter these in the county fair this year. Bet you'd walk away with first prize."

Sara wrinkled her brow. "The country fair? When is it?"

"In August, not far away."

"Oh." Would she still be here in August? She hoped not.

Molly's eyes lighted. "What a great idea. Jackson always enters a couple of quarter horses in the competition. Right, Jackson?"

"Oh, yeah," Jackson said. "Wouldn't miss it."

"And Phil always enters the log rolling contest," Molly went on.

Phil hooked his thumbs under his suspenders. "Took first last year."

"And I'm ridin' a bronc in the rodeo," Buck said.

The light in Molly's eyes vanished. "Oh, Buck, you said you wouldn't ride this year. It's so dangerous. With our baby coming..."

Buck waved a hand. "Now, darlin', don't you worry your pretty little head. Ol' Buck here is, what do you call it...in-vincible."

Sandy guffawed. "That's a mighty big word, Buck. Sure you know what you're talking about?"

Buck didn't answer, but turned to his wife instead. "We'll discuss it later, okay?"

An awkward silence descended on the group. Sara wished she could think of something that would help to clear the air, especially when her cookies had started the discussion. But she was at a loss what to say.

Finally, Phil cleared his throat and said, "We was talkin' about Sara's cookies."

"Right," Sandy said. "And I say she should enter them in the fair."

"Here! Here!" the others chimed in.

Sara's stomach twisted into a knot. "The fair sounds like fun, and I'm flattered you think my cookies could win a prize, but I won't be here then."

"Your memory's comin' back, is it?" Phil said.

"No," Molly said, "it's not. Least, that's what she said while we were fixing lunch."

"My memory's not the problem," Sara said, then added, "I mean, no matter what, I'll be on my own by then."

"So cookin' here at the ranch ain't good enough for you?" Sandy grimaced.

"No, that's not it, either," Sara said. This was going from bad to worse. She looked at Jackson, raising her eyebrows to telegraph, "Help me."

Jackson gave a slight nod, and then said, "Sara's stay here is only temporary. That's been our agreement from the start. Whether or not she gains back her memory, she'll be leaving when she saves up enough money to strike out on her own. That's the situation, gentlemen. Now, it's time we all get back to work."

Chapter Nine

"Hey, Sara, where are you?" Jackson called.

"I'm out here on the front porch."

She'd been sitting on the log sofa for the last half-hour. With the soft breeze, the pots of cheerful flowers, and the weeping willow tree, the porch usually provided a pleasant and peaceful rest, but not today.

Today, Sara's mind was thick with worry. In the past week, she'd finally begun to relax after the ordeal of meeting Mr. Howard. Now, the new threat of seeing a hypnotist had her nerves in a knot again.

The screen door creaked as Jackson opened it and stepped onto the porch. "Getting a little afternoon sun, huh?"

"I guess."

Moving aside a cushion, he sat beside her.

His nearness put her senses on alert. After a day's work, he always radiated fresh air and earth, mixed with his own masculine essence. Heady stuff.

"You look upset," he said, twisting his head to peer at her face. "Did the guys bother you at lunch? If so, I'm sorry. They get carried away, sometimes. But they sure did like your cookies." He grinned.

Sara smiled at the memory of how fast the cookies disappeared. "I'm glad they enjoyed them. But, no, I'm just resting. Dinner's in the oven."

"I thought I smelled roast beef on the way through the kitchen."

"Right. The way you like it, with mashed potatoes and country gravy."

"Great."

"I did some dusting this afternoon and a load of laundry."

"You're really on the job. When Anna returns, I'll have to tell her she has some serious competition."

She raised a hand in protest. "Please, don't! Taking away her job was never my intention."

"Nor mine, either. I was just kidding. But, if she returns before you're ready to move on, you won't have to give up your job. There's enough work around here for both of you. Molly and Buck's baby is due in a few weeks, and she'll need help. Anna would make a fine nanny. Anyway, don't worry."

"Sorry, I guess I'm a bit jumpy today."

Just then, Bingo ambled up the steps and parked himself at Jackson's feet. He looked up at his master with beseeching eyes.

Jackson gave the dog an affectionate pat on the head. "Hey, boy, how ya doin'?"

Sara took advantage of the interruption to make her escape. If she stuck around, Jackson might bring up the subject of the hypnotist. "I'd better see about dinner." She scooted to the edge of the seat.

He laid a hand on her arm. "Can you wait a minute? I have something to tell you."

Oh oh, too late. Her stomach tensed. "I guess I can. What is it?"

"Molly told me about a hypnotist, Marcia Gonzales."

"Molly told me about her, too, and I know what you're going to suggest. But I don't want to see a hypnotist just now." There. She hoped that would put the matter to rest.

But he nodded and went on. "Molly said as much. Why not, Sara? Don't you want to know who you are so you can return to your old life? Your real life?"

Sara dipped her head and wrapped her arms

84

around her waist. "I don't know. I'm so confused."

"I understand, but I've already called Dr. Gonzales and made an appointment for you. Next Wednesday at two o'clock."

Sara's head shot up and heat flooded her cheeks. "You what? How could you? You had no right." He was just like her father, taking matters into his own hands without letting her make the decision.

Jackson drew back. "I was only trying to help."

"Like I couldn't make a call on my own?"

"Of course, you could. I just thought I'd save you the trouble."

Jackson's so-called trying to help raised many bad memories. She realized her father's order to marry Grayson wasn't the only reason she'd run away. She'd fled also because of situations just such as this.

"I'll go with you," Jackson said. "Afterward, we'll do some shopping then have dinner."

More than anything, she wanted to shout, "I'm not going," but taking a stand probably wouldn't make a difference. Resisting never changed her father's mind. He forged ahead with his plans like a bulldozer clearing land for one of his shopping centers. She had thought Jackson was different than her father, but apparently not. Maybe all men were the same, always wanting to be boss.

What good reason did she have for not seeing the hypnotist, anyway? If she put up too much of a fuss, Jackson was sure to get suspicious, as Molly had this afternoon.

Sara's world threatened to collapse. Her runaway attempt failed and the fake amnesia had only worsened the situation. Tears filled her eyes.

Jackson bent closer. "Hey, there. It's okay."

Her anger of a few moments ago gave way to fear as the tears spilled over and rolled down her cheeks. "Oh, Jackson, I'm so scared!"

He put his hands on her shoulders, then turned her around and wrapped her in his arms.

She shouldn't be there, but had no power to move. She let him hold her, and allowed the tears to flow like water released from a dam. At last, she could speak again. "I'm sorry."

"Don't be. Giving in to crying can sometimes be helpful." He pulled a folded handkerchief from a jeans pocket. "Here. I think you need this."

Sara leaned back, took the cloth, and dabbed her wet face. The handkerchief smelled of his aftershave, a pleasant, masculine scent. "Thanks."

"Do you want to talk about why you're so scared?"

Sara bit her lip. Even though she wasn't allowed to talk about her feelings with her father, she was tempted to take Jackson up on his offer. Still, she must be guarded, lest she slip and give away her secret.

"What if my old life is something I don't want to go back to? What if it's a bad life?"

"Then you'll make changes."

"What if I can't?"

"That's hard to believe, Sara. You're an intelligent, capable young woman."

She wiped her eyes again, and then twisted the handkerchief into a spiral. "What if I'm a criminal running away from a crime?" She glanced at him in time to see his mouth quirk. "You think it's funny?"

"So far-fetched as to be humorous, yes."

"How can you be so sure? You don't know me."

"I may not know much about your past, but I know you're not a criminal. No way. If you were, why didn't you just rob me blind and take off? There's plenty of stuff around here you could hock or fence. You could've run off and hitched a ride out of the area."

He had a valid point. "I hadn't thought of it that

way."

"Besides, tell me, in your heart of hearts, do you honestly believe you're a bad person?"

"No..."

He reached up and ran a finger down her cheek, catching a tear she'd missed with the cloth. Her skin tingled under his touch.

"Then set your mind at ease. And, hey, don't think I'm trying to get rid of you. Having you here is a good deal for me. I eat like a king."

She gave a wry laugh. "I'm glad you like my cooking, anyway."

"Sara, look at me." Jackson took her face in both hands.

Slowly, she looked up and met his gaze. Her breath caught at the solemn look in his eyes.

"It's more than that, and you know it." His gaze shifted as he focused on her lips.

"Yes, I do," she murmured, knowing where this sudden intimacy was headed, knowing also they shouldn't go there, but powerless to prevent it.

Jackson leaned closer. "I shouldn't do this," he whispered, "but I can't help myself."

His lips closed over hers, softly, gently. Sara gave an inward sigh. His kiss was a sweet, healing balm, filling her with warmth and tenderness.

She raised a hand to his shoulder, relishing the strength and solidity of his body under her fingers. Like his kiss, his nearness sustained and comforted her. She parted her lips, allowing him to slip his tongue inside to mingle with hers. A warm, delicious sensation filled her.

His arms tightened and he eased her back against the cushions. His mouth left hers and trailed moist kisses along her neck to the V of her throat.

She clasped him around the neck and returned his kiss with all her heart and soul.

Jackson fumbled with the buttons on her blouse.

"Oh, Sara, what you do to me..."

She imagined his fingers, so gentle, so tender, caressing her breast, down over her stomach, wherever he might choose to let them wander, bringing her untold pleasure and joy. No denying she desperately wanted him.

The top button of her blouse sprang free. He filled the gap with his mouth. His tongue moved in slow, enticing circles over her soft flesh.

Sara shivered with delight. Yet, conflict split her apart.

To go on? Or to stop?

You can't do this. You must stop before it's too late!

Despite the voice of reason, she needed all her resolve to put her hands against his chest and carve some distance between them.

"No, Jackson, please!" For a moment, she thought he would ignore her plea, but then he stopped caressing her and sat up. The disappointment reflected in his eyes made her want to cry again.

"Oh, Jackson, I'm sorry, really I am. But we promised ourselves and each other to not get involved like this."

He blew out a deep breath. "I know. Trying to comfort you really started something, didn't it? But, I promise you, we're not going any farther."

Although his voice carried a comforting conviction, Sara wasn't sure she could make the same promise. The way she felt right now, with heat and longing still surging through her, she might be the one to lose control next time. "I shouldn't bother you with my problems," she said. "You've already done so much. I really, really appreciate everything."

"I know you do." He grasped her chin and raised her face. "Come on, don't look so glum. Give me one of your great smiles."

Although she didn't feel the least bit happy, Sara let the corners of her mouth tip up.

"That's better."

"And now, I must check on dinner," she finally said. "Before the roast gets ruined."

He grinned, but grasped her arm as she attempted to rise. "Good idea. But we didn't finish our discussion."

Her stomach knotted. "I'd rather not talk about it anymore."

"Okay. I'll leave it up to you whether or not to see the hypnotist. Think it over and let me know tomorrow, because that's the latest I can cancel the appointment."

****

In his office later that evening, Jackson booted up his computer to make some bookkeeping entries. Concentration eluded him as the memory of Sara's lips on his burned like a bright, hot flame.

He traced his lower lip with his forefinger. Okay, so once again he'd given in to his desire and kissed her. And, okay, maybe he'd pushed a little. But he'd backed off when she'd asked him to.

Keeping his word was no easy task. Not when just the sight of her set his imagination churning with scenes of hot, passionate love.

Why was she so upset about the appointment with the hypnotist? He could understand her misgivings about discovering her past. Yet, he would think the need, the desire to know would spur her on to find out the truth.

Apparently not.

Was something else bothering Sara? Something she hadn't told him? He recalled at least a couple of times when she'd been about to tell him something, only to back off.

The screen before him dimmed to the screensaver and Jackson groaned. His thoughts sidetracked him from his work. He needed to get on with the task at hand.

As he took out an envelope of receipts to enter into the computer, his gaze slid to the small photograph of Cathleen sitting nearby. She'd had it taken on a birthday, especially for him. Looking at her dear, familiar face brought a wave of guilt. When she passed away, he'd sworn never to love another woman with the passion he'd had for her.

And now? Was his promise still true? Or had his feelings for Sara pushed it aside?

"Don't worry," he whispered to the image in the photo, "no one will ever take your place."

****

"Won't you have a seat?" Marcia Gonzales gestured to a sofa and several overstuffed chairs in one corner of her spacious office.

Sara crossed the room and sat in one of the chairs. Instead of leaning back into the cushion, she kept her back rigid.

Dr. Gonzales aimed her gaze at Sara's fingers clutching her purse. "Try to relax, Sara. I promise you this isn't going to hurt."

Sara mustered a weak smile. Distress over this visit had plagued her since she'd told Jackson she would keep the appointment.

She'd had no choice. Rather than raise suspicions, she could only hope she'd somehow get through this meeting with her secret intact.

Dr. Gonzales picked up a pen and clipboard from her desk and sat in a chair across from Sara.

The woman looked every inch the professional in a navy suit and white blouse. Her dark hair was swept off a high forehead and curled around her ears. Fingernails painted a bright red matched her lipstick. She smiled at Sara. "Let's spend some time getting to know each other. I'll go first." She told Sara where she had studied hypnotism and her methods of treatment.

"I never force an issue," Dr. Gonzales said. "The key is to probe and suggest and get you to bring things to consciousness. Now, why don't you tell me something you know about yourself?" The doctor chuckled. "I know the question seems stupid, given you've lost your memory, but anything will be helpful."

Sara licked her dry lips. "Well, when I woke up in the hospital here in Red Rock, they told me I'd been mugged." True enough.

Dr. Gonzales wrote on her clipboard. "How did you feel when you woke up?"

"Let's see...scared. My head hurt where I hit the wall. Where they said I hit the wall," she amended. She reached up to touch the ridge where the stitches had been.

"Okay, think about yourself, not about who you might be, but who you are. What impressions come to mind?"

"I'm not sure what you mean."

"For example, are you a happy person?"

"I don't know." Sara shifted in the chair.

"Okay." Dr. Gonzales tapped her pen against her chin. "Have you discovered anything in particular you're good at?"

"I like to cook." The thought of her favorite activity brought a smile to her lips.

The doctor made a note.

She asked a few more, similar questions, to which Sara answered as truthfully as she could without giving herself away.

Finally, the doctor put down her pen and studied Sara. "You really don't want to be here, do you?"

"Ah, no, I guess I don't."

"Any idea why?"

Sara lowered her eyelids. "I'm not sure. Maybe

I'm afraid of what I might find out."

"That's understandable," the doctor said, her tone more gentle than before.

"I came because Jackson wanted me to."

"I see." She paused. "Well, Sara, even though I understand where you're coming from, my experience has been that if a person resists this kind of therapy, it won't work. I'd be happy to try to help you, but I need your cooperation. Your desire."

Sara bit her lip and blinked back tears that hovered behind her eyes. "I'm sorry I've wasted your time."

The doctor waved a hand. "Not at all. Hopefully, I've given you something to think about." She stood. "I'll keep your information on file, and when you're ready, contact me again, okay?"

"Thank you. I will." Sara exhaled a relieved breath.

The doctor saw her out. As though she'd been set free from a prison, Sara rushed into the waiting room.

Jackson put down the magazine he'd been reading and stood. "How'd it go?" he asked, looking at Dr. Gonzales.

"I'll let Sara tell you about it," she said.

"You weren't in there very long," Jackson said, when they'd left the office and were outside. "Did she hypnotize you?"

Sara gulped in the fresh air. "She never got that far. She interviewed me and decided I wasn't a good candidate." Thank goodness.

"Really? That's too bad." Jackson guided her by the elbow to his truck. "So, how'd you leave it?"

"She said to come back when I'm ready."

"What exactly does that mean?"

"I'm not sure." Seeing his disappointed look, she added, "I'm sorry. You went to a lot of trouble to set this up. I'll pay you back out of my salary."

He waved a hand. "Never mind the trouble or the cost. The important thing is to get your memory – and your life - back."

"I know." Sara looked away. Of course, that would be his highest priority. Once her memory returned, she wouldn't have to stay at the ranch anymore.

But, wasn't that what she wanted, too? To leave the Rolling R and be on her own again?

Chapter Ten

Here, try this one." Sara held out a cookie to
Rose, who sat at the kitchen table. Rose's job-
training period was finally over and she'd come
home for the weekend. Sara welcomed her visit.
Although she and Molly had become good friends,
she felt a special bond with Rose for rescuing her
that fateful night at the train station.

Rose took a bite of the cookie. She chewed a
moment, and then said, "This is delicious. I taste
peppermint, right?"

Sara nodded. "Peppermint is the latest variation
of my basic recipe. I have several different kinds
now."

"I'm impressed. You're a regular cookie factory.
You do great on meals, too. Those lamb chops you
made last night were wonderful, especially the
sauce."

"Thanks."

Rose tilted her head. "Any idea where you
learned to cook so well?"

Before Sara could think what she was saying,
she blurted, "At a gourmet cooking school."

Rose's jaw dropped. "You've remembered
something!"

Sara's entire body tensed. Oh, oh, she'd slipped
again. She pasted on what she hoped was a
bewildered look. "I have?"

"Well, sure. You just said you learned to cook at
a gourmet cooking school."

Sara rubbed her forehead. "I did?"

"Don't tell me you've forgotten what you said

only a few moments ago?"

"I don't know. My head is kind of fuzzy."

Rose leaned forward, her gaze intent. "Can you recall anything else? Where the school was? How you came to go there? Think, Sara. Try to remember."

"I - I'm sorry, Rose." Sara rubbed her forehead harder. "I'm getting a headache."

Rose sat back. "I shouldn't pressure you. Forget about it for now."

Both women were silent awhile, and then Rose stood and carried her coffee mug to the pot for a refill. "Has my brother been treating you okay?"

Now that the subject had changed, some of Sara's tension seeped away. Still, she'd better be on the alert. "He's been very kind."

"I'm glad to hear that. I remember you were worried he didn't want you to stay here."

Guilt over how that situation had changed kept her from meeting Rose's gaze. "He's made me feel more than welcome."

He's made me feel other emotions, too.

From the refrigerator, Sara took a bowl of peas she'd shelled earlier and added them to the chicken soup simmering on the stove. "He can be a pretty nice guy when he wants to."

Rose returned to the table, sat, and picked up another cookie. "How do you like life on the ranch?"

"I like it a lot. The area is beautiful and peaceful. And there's always something interesting going on. Like when Jenny had her foal. Jackson got me out of bed that morning and took me to the barn to see it."

At the memory, she closed her eyes momentarily. Standing beside Jackson, with the soft light from a just-risen sun casting a golden glow on the colt and its mother, had indeed been an experience she'd never forget.

"I like the ranch, too." Rose said. "But I've always had a yen for traveling, which is why I wanted the job with the railroad."

"Is it living up to your expectations?"

"Very much." Rose's eyes shone. "I love meeting all the people."

Rose was in the middle of an amusing anecdote about one of the train's chefs when Jackson came in. Time stood still while Sara covertly watched him take off his hat and hang it on the rack, then exchange his boots for indoor shoes. He looked more handsome and appealing than ever.

He turned in their direction, his gaze focusing on her. "Ladies."

Sara's heart skipped a beat. Her cheeks felt warmer than her work in the kitchen warranted. He always had this effect on her. Even if only a few hours had passed since she'd seen him, when he walked into the room, she'd fall apart inside. "Hey, Jackson," she managed to say, then turned to the stove and vigorously stirred the chicken soup.

"Hello, Brother," Rose said.

"You two having a good visit?" Jackson crossed to the coffee maker and poured himself a cup.

Sara held her breath, expecting Rose to tell him about the gourmet cooking school. Fear kept her from looking at Rose, fear that the truth might be all too evident on her face.

"Yes, and I'm very impressed with Sara's cooking, especially these cookies." Rose nodded at the plate on the table.

Sara expelled her breath and let her shoulders relax. Rose had either forgotten the incident or was keeping it to herself.

Jackson pulled out a chair next to his sister and sat. He helped himself to a cookie. "Me, too." He raised his eyebrows at Sara. "How many versions of these do you have now?"

"Six."

"Six?" Rose's eyes widened.

Jackson nodded. "And I'm helping to name them. There's Chocolate Chewies, Coconut Delights, Peppermint Dreams—and we're still working on the other three."

"Jackson's good with names," Sara put in.

"You ought to enter one recipe in the county fair next month," Rose propped her elbows on the table.

"That's what the crew and I told her," Jackson said.

"I might not be here then," Sara reminded them.

"True," Rose conceded. "Especially if you have any more memory spurts."

"What memory spurts?" He looked from Sara to Rose.

"Sara remembered something about a cooking school," Rose said. "Just a few minutes ago."

"Really? Tell me," he said to Sara.

Sara stopped stirring and sucked in a breath. Not trusting herself to relate the incident without giving away her secret, she said, "I, ah, why don't you tell him, Rose?"

"Okay." Rose related the incident to Jackson.

"Wow!" He sat forward, eyes alert. "The first real breakthrough."

"Maybe," Sara said.

"Why do you say that?" he asked.

"I could have been making it up. I get confused, sometimes."

He nodded. "Okay, but I'm taking it as progress."

"Me, too," echoed Rose.

No one said anything. Sara could only imagine what the two were thinking. Maybe she should tell the truth now and save herself further embarrassment.

Then Rose said, "Hey, Jackson, what about the

grange dance this weekend?"

Sara briefly closed her eyes. Thank you, Rose, for changing the subject.

"What about it?" He reached for another cookie.

"You're going, aren't you?"

"Haven't decided yet."

"You've told Sara about it?"

Jackson's gaze slid sideways to Sara. "Did I? Can't remember. Guess it's my turn to have a memory lapse." His laugh sounded hollow.

He didn't want her to know about it. He didn't want to be obligated to ask her to go, and he was too polite to admit he was going with the others. A heaviness centered in Sara's chest. She casually waved a hand to cover the hurt. "That's okay. Going to a dance is not something I'd want to do."

"Of course, you would!" Rose countered. "Besides, I don't want to go by myself."

Jackson shifted in his chair to face Sara. "The crew will be going, even Molly, though I doubt she'll do much dancing. But Buck plays in the band, so I'm sure she'll come along."

"With all due respect to them, it's not the same as having your company, Jackson. Or yours." Rose nodded at Sara.

Sara wished she could tell them she already had plans to do something else.

But, of course, she didn't have plans. She gave them the best excuse she could muster. "I probably can't dance."

"Maybe you can," Rose said. "But if not, you can sit with Molly. She'll appreciate the company." She crossed her arms over her chest with an air of finality. "I want you both to attend with me."

****

Later, Jackson sat on the porch drinking his after-dinner coffee. Usually, he enjoyed listening to the soft quacking of ducks in the nearby pond, smelling the sweetness of apples ripening on the tree, watching the Colorado sky change from blue to purple to velvety black.

Tonight, guilt colored everything a dull gray. Darn his sister, anyway. He was glad to see her and pleased she'd come home for a visit, but there she was, pushing something on him, as usual.

The last time, bringing Sara home from the hospital had been her mission.

Now, she wanted him to take Sara to the grange dance.

Rose's request shouldn't have been such a big deal, but it was. If he escorted Sara, he'd be expected to dance with her, wouldn't he? Dancing meant taking her in his arms. Smelling her fragrant hair. Feeling the softness of her body against his.

In the end, being miserable because all he could do was dance with her, when he wanted to do much more. So very much more.

She remembered something about her past tonight, something about a cooking school. But the memory upset her, and she'd been reluctant to elaborate. He understood that she wouldn't want to get her hopes up, only to be disappointed.

Yet, even this tiny breakthrough was encouraging. Any time now, her memory might return in full. Maybe even before the dance this weekend. Dare he hope that might be the case?

The door opened, and Rose, carrying a cup of coffee, stepped onto the porch. "I offered to help Sara, but she insisted I relax and enjoy my visit."

Jackson grunted.

Rose sat on the swing. For a couple of minutes, the only sounds were the creaking of the swing as she rocked it with her foot, and the chirping of crickets in nearby bushes. Then she finally spoke. "Why the big pout?"

"Why do you think?" he said.

"You remind me of when we were kids and you didn't get your way. Sometimes, you'd pout for days."

"This is way different. You just can't see that."

After a couple more creaks of the swing, Rose said, "Did you plan to go to the dance and leave Sara home by herself?"

"No. I wasn't planning to go, either."

"Now, that would be a bummer for both of you."

Ignoring her sarcasm, he sipped his coffee. The brew had turned cold, but he drank it anyway.

Rose stopped the swing with her toe and peered at him. "Something's happening between you and Sara."

"What do you mean?"

"You're falling for each other."

"Don't be ridiculous."

"It's obvious to me. For one thing, you can't keep your eyes off each other for more than a couple minutes."

He waved a hand. "Okay, so we're attracted to each other. So what? She's not available and neither am I. We're both clear on that. Attending the dance together would only add fuel to the fire."

Rose started the swing again. "Maybe not. Think of all the men there for Sara to meet. Get someone else interested in her and you'll be off the hook."

"I hadn't thought of that." Would Rose's idea be a way out of this terrible dilemma?

"Since you're unwilling—not ready, rather—to move on with your personal life..."

"Even if I were, I wouldn't choose Sara. She may already be taken. When her memory returns, she'll leave."

"If her memory returns."

Almost too surprised to speak, he stared at his sister. He hadn't considered the possibility Sara's amnesia might be permanent. "Hey, she had a breakthrough tonight. The door to the past opened a crack."

"Maybe." Rose drained her coffee cup. "But if not, she'll have to continue as Sara, won't she?"

"This is sure a different tune than when you wanted me to bring her here. 'Oh, she'll get her memory back soon,' you said."

"So? Maybe I was wrong. And maybe there's hope for both of you."

He shook his head, wishing she'd leave his personal life alone. "I don't want to act like there is when it's a lost cause."

She shrugged. "Okay, so you're both stuck."

"Right." He let a beat of silence go by and then added, "I wouldn't think you'd want to go to the dance, either, since Mike will be there."

Rose lifted her chin. "Unlike you, I'm not stuck. I've already moved on. Therefore, Mike's presence doesn't matter one way or the other."

He wanted to ask what had gone wrong between them in the first place. Although she knew everything about his personal life, somehow, it didn't work the other way around. Besides, if their relationship truly was over, why make her bring up bad memories?

However, neither did he want to sit here and discuss his love life any further. He set down his cup, stood, and stretched. "I have a couple of chores to do," he said, and headed for the steps.

"Think about what I said, Jackson," Rose called out.

****

The grange dance had been underway for about an hour when Jackson found himself sitting all alone at the table he and his group had claimed. He sipped a beer and tried in vain to ignore Sara and her partner whirling around the dance floor.

He needn't have worried about being obligated to dance with her. There had been no opportunity,

101

even if he'd wanted to. Since the music started, one guy after another had claimed her. The current partner was Hal Foster, a local accountant.

Hal had taken Sara off to the side to show her the dance steps. She wore one of the fancy outfits she'd bought the day she and Jackson had shopped in Red Rock, after the trauma of meeting Mr. Howard. A fringed brown vest covered a clingy white top, and a matching skirt showed a lot of leg between the hem and her boots. True to his earlier thought, she had gorgeous legs.

As Hal twirled her under his arm, her vest flew open, revealing rounded breasts under the snug-fitting top. Jackson's temperature shot up a couple of notches. When Hal moved behind her and put his hands on her hips to show her another step, Jackson gritted his teeth.

"You look lonesome over here all by yourself," said a feminine voice. "Want some company?"

Jackson looked around to see Trisha Morgan. He didn't really want company, and he'd already danced with her once this evening, but common courtesy obliged him to say, "Sure, Trisha, sit down."

Trisha slid onto a folding chair. Her perfume wafted his way, a scent too sweet for his taste. "I'll keep Rose's seat warm until she comes back."

Rose was dancing with Bob Hoffmann, who owned B & H Feed. She had spoken to Mike when he'd arrived, and then ignored him. Jackson couldn't worry about Rose and her affairs, though. He couldn't get his mind—or his gaze—off Sara.

"So, how're things at the Rolling R?" Trisha asked.

"Just fine, thanks." Jackson drummed his fingertips on the table.

"Heard your new cook lost her memory. I can't imagine what that would be like."

"Not fun, from what I've seen."

Hal and Sara returned to the dance floor. Sara's face was flushed and she was smiling, like she was having a great time. Well, good for her.

"What happened to your other cook, Anna Gabraldi?" Trisha asked.

"She's taking care of her grandkids while her daughter and husband visit a sick relative."

Hal and Sara danced toward them. Not wanting Sara to catch him watching her, Jackson turned sideways and focused on Trisha. Besides, he felt guilty for not paying her more attention. But, if she'd noticed his preoccupation, she wasn't letting on.

She took a sip of wine, smiling at him over the rim of her glass.

With her dark hair and big, round eyes, she really was pretty. "How are things at the bank?" he asked.

"Same old, same old. I'm thinking about applying for a similar job in Denver. Kind of tired of our little ol' town."

"I'd be sorry to see you leave."

Her eyes widened. "You would?"

"Well, sure. I mean, you've lived here all your life..." Darn, he'd better watch what he said. He didn't want to give her the impression he took a personal interest in whether or not she remained in Red Rock.

He wished some of the others would return to the table, but Buck was playing his fiddle in the band, of course, and Molly had moved closer to the bandstand. Sandy joined some cronies from a neighboring ranch. Phil was hustling a woman Jackson didn't know. Diego had disappeared with his new girlfriend, Maria.

The music stopped just as Hal and Sara waltzed up to the table. "I'd like to sit down for a while," Sara said.

Hal wrinkled his forehead, but said, "Okay." He

was a tall, rangy man with a pencil-thin mustache. "Catch you later." He held out a hand to Trisha. "How 'bout it, gal?"

Trisha glanced at Jackson.

"Go for it," he said.

"Sure." Trisha rose and took Hal's hand. The music began and they danced off.

Sara slipped into her chair. She picked up her wineglass and took a sip.

"Having fun?" Jackson asked.

"Yes. I don't know the fancy steps, but I seem to be okay with a basic two-step and swing. How about you? Are you having fun?"

He straightened and pasted a cheerful smile on his face. "Sure am."

"It's a nice place."

He followed her sweeping gaze of the room. He wasn't sure he'd call the grange hall "nice," although tonight the streamers and balloons hanging from the rafters, and the bales of hay and a wheelbarrow full of flowers on the bandstand added a festive touch. At one end, a portable bar sat next to a buffet table loaded with food. The aromas of barbecued ribs, baked beans, and roasted corn filled the air.

"It's an old building," he said. "At first, only ranchers used it, but now other groups meet here, too."

"That's interesting."

He glanced at her and his heart skipped a beat. Flushed from dancing, her face had a pink glow, and little tendrils of damp hair clung to her cheeks and forehead.

At the point of asking if she wanted more wine, he glimpsed Cal Martin, Red Rock's veterinarian, headed their way. He'd heard about Cal's recent divorce from a wife who decided she didn't like small town life.

Cal's gaze was glued to Sara, leaving no doubt

what was on his mind.

Which would be worse - to endure the agony of watching her dance with Cal, or to face the temptations brought by dancing with her himself? He had only a split second in which to decide.

He jumped up, grabbed Sara's hand, and pulled her to her feet. "Come on, let's dance." The words came out rougher than he'd intended, but Cal was closing in.

Sara's eyes widened, but she followed him to the dance floor.

As they passed Cal, Jackson gave him a smile and a nod.

Cal returned the nod, but pursed his lips instead of smiling.

Jackson pulled Sara into his arms, a bit tighter than he intended. But the floor was crowded and he needed to maneuver them around without bumping into people. Or so he told himself. She was graceful and light on her feet, just as he'd imagined she would be, from the first time he'd watched her move around his kitchen.

Her hair, full of an herbal shampoo scent, brushed his cheek like strands of the softest satin. Her small hand lay nestled in his, while her hips, firm and round, moved sensuously under his careful guidance.

"I see your sister is dancing with Dr. Mike," she said. "But they don't look happy."

He roused himself from his thoughts to let the words sink in. "Really?" He glanced at the couple. Yes, they were dancing together, but both were grim-faced and gazing into space.

"Is something going on between those two?"

"There was. Rose never told me what went wrong."

"Too bad, especially if they still care for each other."

"I've suspected they do. Yes, it is too bad when people who care for each other can't work out their problems." His stomach tensed as the words took on a new meaning.

He looked down and met her gaze. The intense blue of her eyes at such close range snatched away his breath. His chest felt heavy, his throat choked. His gaze slid to her lips, moist and soft-looking. So near. What if he kissed her, right there on the dance floor, with everyone as witnesses?

"Sometimes solving a problem is beyond a person's control," she said, her voice solemn.

"Don't you believe the old saying, 'True love conquers all'?"

"I'm not sure."

They had ceased talking about Rose and Mike and were talking about the two of them. He knew it, and knew she did, too. Instead of saying anything more, he gritted his teeth and steered them into a turn.

Chapter Eleven

"How about getting some fresh air?" Jackson asked Sara when the song ended. "There's a garden out back."

"I'd like that."

Outside, relieved to be free of the crowded dance floor, Sara breathed in the cool, evening air. Overhead was an ebony sky full of glittering stars, a sight she rarely saw in the city. She loved the way the moonlight etched everything in silver.

They stepped onto an asphalt path where ground level light globes illuminated flowerbeds and wooden benches. The scent of roses filled the air. Sara had attended dances in much more elegant surroundings, but, somehow, they paled in comparison to the grange's garden.

After strolling awhile in silence, he asked, "So, are you still having a good time?"

Jolted by his accusing tone, she glanced up and saw him staring straight ahead, his jaw set. "Yes, I am. I'm glad I know how to dance at least some of the steps. Otherwise, you'd have a wallflower on your hands."

"You've hardly been that. In fact, if we were in the Old South, you'd be the belle of the ball."

"People here are very friendly."

"Especially Hal Foster."

He stuck out his chin, as though daring her to deny Hal had been a frequent partner tonight. Then it dawned on her - he was jealous.

A tingle of satisfaction slid down her spine. She hadn't set out to make him jealous, but now that he was, she couldn't help but gloat a little. "Hal seems like a nice person."

"For a bean counter, he's okay. But he didn't need to monopolize you tonight."

"He didn't. I danced with others, too."

"Not with me."

"We just finished dancing," she said, suppressing a smile.

"Once."

"But you were with Trisha. And Hal said—"

"Hal said what?"

"That you and Trisha were close."

"Close? What the hell did he mean? Why, that dirty, no-good..." He made a fist and pounded his other palm. "We've gone out a few times is all."

"Oh."

A wave of relief washed over Sara. She had thought Hal's observation odd, given what she knew about Jackson's lingering feelings for his former fiancée. "Trisha is pretty."

"Not as pretty as you." His voice deepened, all traces of annoyance gone. A couple beats of silence slid by, then he said, "Come on, let's sit here."

He led them to a bench near a rose garden. The sweet scent of the flowers floated by on the night breeze. As they sat, he edged close to her, sliding one arm along the back of the bench.

Sara's heart beat faster. She should move away, but an intense desire to remain close rooted her in place.

Jackson cupped her chin and turned her face toward him. Moonlight shone on his cheekbones, the ridge of his nose, the square angle of his jaw. When she looked into his eyes and saw the depth of emotion, her breath caught.

"As far as I'm concerned, you're the only woman here I care about dancing with."

She felt the same way about him. The one dance

they'd shared had been the only one that really mattered.

He traced a finger along her chin. "In fact, you're the only one I care about, period."

His words sent a shiver down her spine, but, at the same time, her heart ached. "Oh, Jackson, you know we can't go down that road. We both have our problems. You're not over your grieving."

A shadow crossed his face. "I know."

"And I have my own dilemma."

"Okay, granted. But if we could go forward, then you'd be the one I'd choose. In a minute."

"And I'd choose you."

"Really?" He gave a low, hungry growl and pulled her into his arms.

Sara knew they'd just done something very dangerous with the "what if" exchange, but she had no willpower to worry about it now. The delicious pleasure of being in his arms made her forget everything. He nuzzled her hair, sending pleasure trickling down the back of her neck. She reached up to touch his cheek, felt the rough stubble of beard under her fingers. He caught her hand, brought it to his lips, and, one by one, kissed each fingertip.

A tidal wave of emotion swept her away. She'd tried so hard to fight her growing feelings, but knew she was losing the battle. Boldly, she lifted her face to his. Their lips hovered only inches apart. His warm breath feathered across her cheek. "Kiss me," she whispered, sensing he waited only for permission.

"Oh, yes."

He gave a low groan, and then covered her mouth with his. After several delightful moments of their lips meshing together, his tongue probed hers apart. She opened her mouth to him and their tongues mingled in a sensuous dance. In the distance, the band inside the hall played on.

Overhead, the stars whirled together in a dizzying kaleidoscope of lights. Being in Jackson's arms was heaven on earth, and the only place she wanted to be.

Long moments later, Sara eased away and nestled against his chest. "It's so pleasant out here. I wish we could stay forever."

"Like those statues over there." He pointed to a couple of stone cherubs on a nearby water fountain.

She giggled. "Well, not exactly like that. I'd like a little more action than they have."

He joined in her laughter. "Me, too."

They were silent while the crickets chirped, and then he said, "Seriously, Sara, I've been giving your problem a lot of thought. You're stuck until your memory returns, and that hasn't happened. Seeing Dr. Gonzales didn't help, so why don't you let me hire a private detective to see if he can find out who you are?"

A private detective? Sara stiffened, panic chasing away her comfort. "Oh no. I don't want you to do that!"

"Why not?"

She groped for a reason. "Because...because it's too expensive."

"I can afford it."

She shook her head. "I'm already indebted to you for so much. No, I can't let you hire a detective."

He peered at her, his eyes serious in the dim light. "Why are you so upset? I thought you wanted to know the truth."

"Yes, of course, I do. I don't know why I suddenly panicked."

He drew her into his arms again and pressed her head against his chest. His hand lingered, caressing her hair with gentle strokes. "Don't worry now. We'll talk about it some other time."

Sara hoped to relax and recapture the joy she'd

experienced moments ago, but his talk about hiring a detective dominated her thoughts. She'd had no business kissing him again, anyway. Playing "what if" with their emotions had been a dangerous mistake.

****

Several days later, Sara put a batch of cookies made from a new recipe in a plastic tub and sealed the lid. At the others' continued urging, she'd decided to enter one of her creations in the county fair's baked goods contest, only a few weeks away. She had yet to choose which version to enter. She was taking these to Molly, hoping that after she'd tasted them, she could help her come to a decision.

Soon after the fair was over, Sara would leave the ranch. By then, she'd have enough money saved to finish her trip to California. She still didn't know what she'd do when she reached her destination, but she was determined to follow through with her plan.

As she slipped the tub into a paper bag, her thoughts turned to Jackson. Since the dance, they had settled back into their routine of boss and employee. More or less. Intimate touching occurred between them more often than before. Sometimes when she stood at the stove, he'd put his arms around her while he peered in the pot to see what was cooking. When they talked, he'd lay a hand on her arm to emphasize something he said. Or, he'd give her a quick kiss on her cheek before she went up to bed. Little things.

At first, she'd held her breath, waiting to see if he would push for more. He didn't, but he clearly intended to take every advantage of what their agreed-upon limits allowed.

This morning, he'd gone to Littleton, to meet a buyer for a couple of his quarter horses. Before leaving, he'd kissed her soundly on the lips. "Take care," he'd said. "I'll be back soon."

Still dreaming about the touch of his warm lips, Sara left the house. Bingo, who'd been lounging under the apple tree, jumped up and ran to her side. She reached down to pat his silky head. "We're going for a walk."

She stopped in the garden to pick a pretty pink rosebud for Molly, who hadn't felt well lately. With the baby due any time, she was uncomfortable and easily fatigued. The recent hot weather hadn't helped.

The Drakes's cottage was only a few minutes away. Today the walk took a little longer than usual because Sara stopped to pick some daisies to add to the rose.

When she reached her destination, she noticed the cottage door was closed. That was odd. On a warm day such as today, Molly kept the door open. Leaving Bingo to nose about the yard, Sara stepped onto the porch. The air was strangely quiet—no Western music played, no pots and pans clanged in the kitchen. A little shiver of foreboding snaked down her spine.

She tapped on the door. "Molly, are you home? It's Sara."

No answer, only an eerie stillness.

After another, louder knock, she thought she heard a noise inside, but Molly didn't come to the door.

The knob turned under her touch, and the door opened. "Molly?"

"H-help," came a feeble voice.

Sara gripped the doorknob. Molly was in trouble.

"Hang on, I'll be right there!"

Sara ran into the house, tossing the flowers and bag of cookies onto the sofa as she passed by. A sprint down the hall brought her to the bedrooms. The voice came from the room Molly and Buck had fixed up for the baby.

At the doorway, Sara barely noticed the colorful wallpaper, the crib with a musical Winnie-the-Pooh mobile, the shelf filled with stuffed animals, all of which she'd oohed and ahhed over on other occasions.

Her gaze riveted instead on the figure lying on the floor.

Molly.

Heart thumping, Sara raced to Molly and knelt beside her. "What happened?"

"Oh, Sara...thank God. I tripped...can't get up. My-my water broke."

For the first time, Sara noticed the pool of liquid seeping from underneath Molly. Fear arrowed through her. What should she do? Try to help Molly get up? Would it hurt the baby? She was at a loss what to do in this situation. She'd always heard about her friends' childbirth experiences after the fact.

"I'll call Buck," she said. "Where's the phone?"

"O-over there." Molly pointed to a cordless phone lying on the diaper-changing table.

Sara snatched up the phone. "What's the number?"

"It's on speed dial." Molly ground out directions from between clenched teeth.

Sara could tell she was in great pain. Her face was as white as the stack of diapers on the changing table, and beads of sweat lined her upper lip. Keeping an anxious eye on Molly, Sara located the number and connected it. She listened to the shrill ringing for several seconds. "He's not answering. Are all the others with Buck?"

Molly managed to nod. "They're in the upper pasture mending fences. Buck's is the only number I have, except for Jackson's." Her face contorted with pain.

"Jackson's gone to Littleton. That's too far away for him to help." Buck's phone switched to voice mail just then, and Sara left a terse message informing him of the situation. "I'll call nine-one-one and have an ambulance sent," she told Molly when she'd finished the call.

"It's—it's too late. Contractions getting closer together...I'm afraid baby's c-coming." Molly breathed out with a loud whoosh.

Sara's heart thumped. "You're sure?"

"Yes! Sara, get me t-to hospital. Can you drive?"

The image of her blue convertible sports car popped into Sara's mind. "I, ah, probably. But—"

"Can you deliver a b-baby?"

"No! I know I can't do that."

"Then drive me...keys in purse...my bedroom."

Sara ran into the adjacent bedroom. Looking frantically around, she spotted a small brown purse on the dresser. She dug into it and located the keys, then called over her shoulder, "Got 'em, Molly. Hang on, I'll be right back."

Hurrying out the front door, she clattered down the steps and headed to the detached garage, where the Drakes's older model compact was stored. The sudden coolness of the dark interior sent a chill over her. Not waiting for her eyes to adjust, she fumbled for the car's door handle, and when she found it, yanked the door open and fell into the driver's seat.

Two minutes later, she pulled the car next to the front porch. Now, how to get Molly into the car? As a brilliant idea struck her, Sara ran to Buck's kitchen cubbyhole office and grabbed the wheel-mounted desk chair. She managed to lift Molly into it. The chair's arms kept her from falling out.

When Sara wheeled Molly out to the porch, the sight of the stairs ground her to a halt. They would have to be negotiated without the chair.

"There are only three steps," Sara said as she

lifted Molly from the chair. "You can manage them. I'll be holding you."

Molly stuck out a foot and eased down a step. "Ohhh," she groaned, and doubled over.

"Rest a bit," Sara advised, "then try the next one."

At last, Molly was down the steps and into the back seat of the car. Sara left her to run into the house for some blankets to build up the floor, so she wouldn't roll off the seat.

Finally, they were on their way. Red Rock was at least twenty minutes away. She hoped the baby would wait until they arrived before entering the world.

At the highway intersection, Sara paused to wait for traffic to clear, and then swung the car onto the highway. Although she hadn't been behind the wheel for a month or more, and never drove much at home, anyway, the hang of it quickly came back. "How're you doing?" she called over her shoulder.

"I - I'm okay, so far," Molly said.

At last, Sara spotted the Red Rock City Limits sign. She wasn't sure she remembered the route to the hospital, but, thankfully, street signs guided them. Soon the Emergency entrance came into view.

She pulled under the portico, jumped from the car, and ran inside. In mere minutes, attendants arrived and took Molly away. After answering a few questions of the admissions person, Sara collapsed into a chair in the lobby. She looked at her hands and saw they were shaking. In fact, her entire insides felt like Jell-O.

Getting Molly to the hospital had been a miracle. If only Buck had been there to help.

Buck.

They'd been in such a hurry neither had thought to leave a note. When Buck either received the voicemail message she'd left or returned and found

Molly gone, he'd probably guess. Still, she needed to assure him they'd reached the hospital okay.

Sara rose and stumbled to a pay phone. Fortunately, she had some coins in her pocket. From phoning Molly numerous times to arrange visits, she knew the Drakes's number by heart. Tapping her fingers, she waited until the answering machine clicked on, and, careful to keep her voice calm and reassuring, left a message. Not having made a mental note of Buck's cell number, she couldn't call again. She knew Jackson's, though, and his phone was always on when he was away from the ranch.

He answered after only a couple of rings.

Pulling herself together, she poured out the events of the past hour.

"You drove Molly to the hospital?" he said.

"Yes. Like I said, we tried to reach Buck, but he wasn't answering his cell. It was either drive her or deliver the baby myself." She gave a mirthless laugh. "I figured driving was the best bet. But, Jackson, Buck should be here. Molly needs him."

And I need you, she wanted to add. She needed his strength, his courage, and his calmness in the face of a crisis.

"I know where he's working today. I'll head home and find him. We'll be there as soon as possible."

After they said good-bye, Sara learned from the receptionist that Molly was still in labor and that Dr. Mike had arrived. With nothing to do but wait, she returned to her seat. She kept her gaze glued to the entrance, and when Jackson and Buck finally strode through the sliding glass doors, a huge wave of relief rolled over her. Teary-eyed, she lurched to her feet, just as Jackson spotted her and rushed to her side.

Buck was close behind him.

"Sara!" Jackson reached out and drew her into

his arms.

"I'm so glad you're here!"

For a moment, she forgot everything but how wonderful Jackson's arms felt around her. Don't ever let me go, she wanted to say.

"Any word yet?" Buck asked.

"Oh, Buck, I'm sorry!" Sara pulled away from Jackson. "I didn't mean to ignore you. Molly's still in labor, but Dr. Mike's with her."

"Then she's in good hands," Jackson said. "But go to her, buddy. She needs you, too."

"Right." Buck turned toward the doors leading to the hospital's interior.

"Give her our love," Jackson called after him. "And tell her we're rooting for her and the baby."

Over dinner in the hospital's cafeteria, Sara related the details she hadn't told him over the phone. "Did you find out why Buck didn't answer his cell?"

He finished a bite of his hamburger. "A calf got caught in the wire fencing. The phone must've somehow come unhooked from his belt while he was rescuing the animal. He was looking for the phone when I found him."

"Did he find it?"

"No, and we didn't want to waste any more time. We took off for Red Rock right away."

"I'm glad he finally got here—and that you did, too."

As their gazes met across the table, an emotion she couldn't put a name to passed between them. She knew only that it reached deep down inside and touched her soul.

When they returned to the hospital's waiting room, they learned a daughter had been delivered, and that mother, father, and baby were doing fine. If they wanted to wait a bit, they could see the baby, and the parents, too.

"Of course, we'll wait," Jackson said, and Sara nodded her agreement.

A short while later, Sara and Jackson went to Molly's room. The new mother, looking tired but happy, lay propped up in bed. Buck sat at her side. They were holding hands and gazing into each other's eyes, while deep in conversation. The baby lay in a bassinet nearby.

When Buck saw them, he sprang to his feet. "Hey, you two!"

Jackson grabbed Buck's hand and pumped it up and down, then clapped him on the back. "Congratulations!"

"Thanks, boss."

Jackson leaned down and kissed Molly's cheek. "How's the little mother?"

Molly smiled. "I'm doing fine. I'm so glad you're here."

While the three friends talked, Sara remained in the background, suddenly feeling like an outsider. Then she caught Molly's gaze over Jackson's shoulder.

"Sara, come join us," Molly said.

Sara crossed to the bed and grasped Molly's outstretched hands. "I'm so glad you're all right."

"Thanks to you, I am. But say hello to our daughter!" Wearing a broad smile, she pointed to the bassinet.

Sara leaned over the bassinet and saw the tiny baby wearing a pink cotton cap, her fist curled above the blanket. Her eyes fluttered open, and then closed in peaceful sleep. Sara's heart filled with emotion. "She's darling."

"What a sweetheart," Jackson said. "I bet she'll have your red hair, Molly."

How lucky Molly and Buck were, to have each other and now a child who was a part of them both. Sara heaved a deep sigh. Would this ever happen to her? Yet how could it, when she had chosen to lie about herself?

Molly said, "I've been telling Buck about how you rescued me."

Buck chimed in, "We sure do thank you, Sara."

Sara turned away from the baby and nodded. "I'm glad I was there to help."

"Have you decided on a name?" Jackson asked.

Molly exchanged a look with her husband. "We were just discussing that. We'd like to call her Karleen Sara Drake. Karleen is Buck's mother's name." She turned to Sara, eyes shining. "And the Sara is for you, of course. Would you mind? We know it's probably not your real name, but to us, you'll always be Sara."

Sara blinked back her sudden tears. "I'd be honored."

Molly and Buck both beamed.

Sara glanced at Jackson. Their gazes met and held. The tenderness there reached out, enveloping her like a warm and protective blanket. She no longer felt like an outsider. For now, she belonged here with these three wonderful people.

No matter what happens in the future, I'll never forget this happy moment.

Chapter Twelve

Later that evening, after Sara had gone to bed, Jackson was too restless to sleep. He went out on the front porch and sat in one of the log chairs. A soft breeze drifted down from the hills. Crickets chirped from their havens in nearby shrubs.

He thought about being in Valley General Hospital today and realized he hadn't felt as depressed there as he usually did. When he'd first walked in, the bad memories churned his stomach. Then, after spotting Sara and taking her into his arms, he'd all but forgotten his discomfort.

He smiled at how happy Buck and Molly were with their new baby. They were a real family now.

As he had gazed at little Karleen, he was filled with a long-buried yearning. A yearning for a wife, and for children. He realized how incomplete his life was, and that a family would make it whole.

Although he'd loved Cathleen, she was gone. Now, Sara was the woman he'd choose to share his life.

The fun they'd have making babies. The hot passion of loving each other. The freedom to exchange kisses and caresses any time they chose and without restriction, because she belonged to him and he to her.

He made a fist and pounded the arm of the chair. How could Sara ever belong to him? She wasn't free. He might choose to move on with his life, but, until her memory returned or until someone claimed her, she was stuck in limbo.

There must be a way out of this dilemma.

Surely, there were other amnesiacs who'd gone on to live full lives without knowing their pasts.

Jackson set his jaw and made a vow. He would not let the past imprison him any longer, nor would he allow it to imprison Sara. He'd wait a few more weeks, until after the county fair. Then, if her situation were still the same, he'd have a serious talk with her about their future.

Feeling much better than when he'd first come out to the porch, Jackson rose and went inside.

Before going upstairs, he entered his office and turned on the desk lamp. He sat in the chair and gazed for long moments at Cathleen's photo. The soft lamplight blurred her features a little, as though he were viewing her across a great distance. He picked up the photo and held it nearer, ran a finger over the section of glass covering her cheek.

"A part of me will always love you," he whispered to the image. "But another part must say good-bye."

He focused on her smile and could have sworn it widened. Jackson gazed at the image for a while longer then opened a drawer and slipped the picture inside. He shut the drawer and turned out the light. Filled with a curious mixture of sadness and happiness, he stood and went to bed.

****

Hands on her hips, Sara studied the array of tops and vests spread across her bed. Which outfit should she wear to the county fair today? Jeans for sure, but what would go with them? The pink blouse was pretty, but she also liked the red T-shirt embroidered with daisies.

"You ready yet?" Jackson's voice floated up from downstairs.

"In a minute."

She considered her choices for a second longer, and then grabbed the pink blouse. When she was dressed, she turned to the mirror and ran a comb through her hair. She spread gloss on her lips, grabbed her Lady Stetson, and headed for the stairs.

Jackson waited at the bottom.

"How do I look?" She twirled around.

Jackson's gaze slid over her body. "You look great. A little like a city dude, but great, just the same."

"Well, I have to wear these dressy clothes I bought sometime. Otherwise, I will have wasted my hard-earned money."

"Hey, I'm not complainin'." He reached out, grasped her by the shoulders, and kissed the tip of her nose.

"You're not so bad yourself," she said when he had released her and she had a chance to look him over. His jeans were new, and he'd added a bolo tie to his light blue shirt.

He took her by the elbow. "Thank you, ma'am. But come on, we'd better be on our way. The others have already left."

"The baby will be okay with Sue Ellen?"

"She's the best nanny I could find. And Molly will be away only a few hours. She's coming home right after Buck's rodeo ride."

"Did you ever do any rodeo riding?" she asked him as they headed outside to his truck.

"A couple of times, when I was a lot younger and a lot more reckless." He grinned. "I decided I'd rather raise horses. On the rodeo circuit, I'd be away too often from the ranch."

"What about Buck, then?"

"He's entering one of the amateur contests for anyone who wants to try his hand."

"I get the impression Molly isn't too happy about his decision."

"Nope. And rightly so. If rodeo gets into his blood, his family life and his work here will be affected." He opened the truck door.

She climbed in and waited until he was in place beside her, then said, "Rodeo must be hard on wives or significant others."

"Yes, a lot of women don't like their men involved. But I can understand the appeal. You get a super rush when you and the horse fly out of the chute. And if you bust him, well, that's icing on the cake."

"I wouldn't want my husband risking his life on a wild horse."

Jackson steered the truck onto the road leading to the highway. "With me, you wouldn't have to worry."

Sara's heart jolted. What was he implying? When he looked in her direction, she met his gaze, her stomach flipping like a flapjack.

"Did you hear what I said?"

"Yes, but..." She was at a loss how to respond. Surely, he wasn't proposing?

Jackson pulled off the road onto the shoulder. He switched off the engine and turned to face her. "No, I'm not proposing," he said, resting his arm along the back of the seat. "But after the fair is over, I planned to have a talk about our future, if we have one. Which I hope we do."

"What exactly did you plan to talk about?"

"I'd like you to start thinking about what you will do if you never regain your memory."

She stiffened. "Oh, Jackson, I don't know..."

"The future is important to me, Sara. Don't my feelings matter?"

"Of course, but—"

He leaned toward her. "I saw a TV show once about an amnesiac woman who was discovered living in Alaska. She'd married and had children and was very happy. She never went back to her old life, even after she found out who she originally was."

"Did she have a husband in her old life?"

"No. But she had parents, siblings, and friends. The point is, a person who loses memory permanently can establish a new life - and be happy."

A wild idea took root in Sara's mind, causing a shiver to run through her. What if she never regained her memory, as far as Jackson and the others were concerned? Could she leave her old life behind, just like that, and take up a new identity?

What about her father? And Grayson? Would disappearing from the face of the earth be fair to them? Wouldn't they soon search for her? She figured her father was punishing her right now by ignoring her absence. At some point, he'd lose patience and begin a search. With his money and resources, she had no doubt he'd find her.

No, continuing her deception would never work.

"Sara?" Jackson touched her shoulder.

"Oh, sorry. What were you saying?"

"That seeing Buck and Molly so happy with little Karleen made me realize I want to move on with my life. If you're not ready yet, I'm willing to wait. But I want you to be thinking about it."

Sara bit her lower lip and remained silent.

Cupping her chin, he ran a fingertip over her lips. "I'm not saying you and I should get together just to make babies, although I'm sure we'd have a great time. I want to be with you for many reasons. You know that."

Jackson's words touched her deep inside. "I know...and, thank you," she whispered.

His gaze searched hers. "Aside from your memory problem, you've been happy here, haven't you?"

"Very happy."

"And you could keep on being happy?"

"I'm sure of it."

Hot tears filled her eyes. Tell him the truth. Right now.

Yet she couldn't. What if he didn't understand? What if her deception angered him? Besides, now was not the time for a confession. The setting had to be just right, and she needed to have in mind exactly what she would say.

She'd wait until the fair was over. Then she'd tell him the truth about herself.

Jackson reached to wipe away her tears. "Hey, hey. I didn't mean to make you cry, honey. I want today to be fun. I should have kept quiet until afterward, like I'd planned."

"Don't worry, I'm fine." She forced a shaky smile.

"Think about what I said, and we'll talk more later."

Leaning toward her, he covered her mouth with his warm lips. Desire and longing spiraled through her. If only they could have a future together.

He drew away and gazed into her eyes. "I love you with all my heart."

Sara's heart leaped. She'd never expected to hear those words from him. At least, not yet. "I love you, too," she whispered over a suddenly dry throat. Their love for each other was real and powerful. She could feel it flowing back and forth between them.

He hugged her again, and then drew away. "We'd better be on our way before I take you back to the house and show you just how strong my feelings are." Jackson started the engine and pulled the truck onto the road. While they drove along, he talked about what they would do at the fair.

Still stunned, she barely focused on his words.

They'd just admitted to being in love.

****

By the time they reached the fairgrounds, Sara had managed to push her dilemma to the back of her mind. Today she would enjoy herself.

As Jackson had told her, first on the agenda was checking the status of her cookies. They located the building housing the baked goods and stepped inside. After strolling by displays of pies, cakes, and biscuits, they finally came to the cookies.

Sara scanned the tiers, looking for her entry. "I see mine!"

"I do, too. And you won first prize!"

Sara stared at the huge blue ribbon hanging above the cookies. "Are you sure it's for my entry?"

"Yes, I'm sure. The poster says so. 'Peppermint Dreams, First Place'." He gathered her close for a hug. "I'm so proud of you. Look out, Mrs. Fields, here comes Sara."

Happiness filled Sara's heart. "I'm glad I can do something well, even if it's only making cookies."

"Hey, don't sell yourself short. Cookies are very important in a person's life. In my life, anyway," he added with a grin.

They looked at the other exhibits and then went to the fairway, where they tested their skills on darts and the shooting gallery. Jackson's careful aim won a plush teddy bear for Sara. They explored the Fun Forest and took a wild roller coaster ride. They sampled roasted peanuts, cotton candy, and chocolate chip ice cream from the concessionaires.

"Having fun?" Jackson asked.

"Most definitely."

"You wouldn't get tired of coming to fairs like this, year after year?"

"Never. Not as long as I'm with you."

An image of the two of them attending the fair with a couple of children in tow popped into Sara's mind. Was such a future really possible?

The more she considered spending the rest of her life with Jackson, the more comfortable she felt. The world took on a new brightness, a new clarity.

Being with him these past couple of months had given her the courage to go forward and create a future that would make her life complete.

"It's about half an hour till Buck's due to ride," Jackson said, "but I'd like to give him some moral support beforehand. Okay?"

"Fine."

On their way to the grandstand, someone called Sara's name. She turned to see Ella Simons, coordinator for the contest she'd entered.

Ella hurried toward them, gray hair from her single braid curling around her face. "Glad I caught you, Sara. There's a photographer from a big magazine back east who wants pictures of our prizewinners. 'Course, if I had known in advance he was coming, I could have set up something. But no, he just breezes in and expects everyone to be available. Anyway, could you come to the exhibit for a few minutes?"

Sara hesitated. While she didn't particularly want her picture taken, chances were slim anyone she knew would be interested in the winners of a country fair baking contest. "Why, I suppose so. Is it okay, Jackson?"

"Go ahead," he said, "then come to the grandstand. I'll check in with Buck then wait for you at the main entrance."

Sara followed Ella to the exhibit building where they joined a small group clustered around the baked goods display.

The photographer, a tall man with spiky blond hair, barked out instructions. "You in the blue jacket, stand over here, and you in the gray hat, over there. The light in this building sucks! Louann, take the light to that corner." The photographer pointed a long finger into the shadows.

Louann? Sara sucked in a breath. She knew a Louann Brougham on Long Island. She belonged to the same country club as the Carletons.

But no, this woman couldn't be that Louann. Not way out here in Colorado.

Then a dark-haired woman holding a fluorescent bar light stepped forward. Tall and as thin as a reed, she wore a stylish brown pants suit. Sara's heart sank. She was indeed Louann Brougham.

What was she doing such a long way from home? And why would wealthy Louann be working as a photographer's assistant?

While the other contest winners chatted about having their pictures in a magazine, Sara shrank back, wishing she could disappear. But if she left now, she would draw attention. There might be a chance Louann wouldn't recognize her. Her clothing was different, for one thing. For another, she wouldn't be expecting to see Sara here, either.

Louann held up the bar light. Just before she turned it on, she looked straight at Sara. A startled look crossed her face and she opened her mouth to speak.

"No, no, the man said, "the light farther left, please, darling."

Louann turned to follow his direction.

Snap, snap, snap. The photographer hopped about, tilting the camera this way and that. In between shots, he kept them on their toes. "You by the pie, smile more! Miss Prize-winning Cake, move your hand away from your ribbon. That's it."

At last he was finished. Sara's heart pounded so hard she could hardly breathe. She needed to leave, and fast. She whirled and found herself directly in the path of Louann Brougham.

"Sara? Sara Carleton? Is that you?"

128

Chapter Thirteen

Sara pasted what she hoped was a blank look on her face. "Beg your pardon?"

Louann tilted her head. "Aren't you Sara Carleton, from Long Island, New York?"

The less she said, the better. "My first name is Sara, but I live here in Colorado."

"No kidding?" Her gaze narrowed. "I would have sworn you're Sara Carleton. You even sound like her."

Sara hadn't considered her voice might give her away and clamped her mouth shut.

"I haven't seen Sara Carleton for a while," Louann went on, adjusting the strap of her fashionable shoulder bag. "Her father said she's on an extended vacation, but it's not like her to go away without telling her friends."

"You'll have to excuse me," Sara mumbled. "I, ah, need to meet someone."

"Oh, sure." Louann took a step backward. "When Sara finally comes home to New York and I tell her she has a double who lives in Colorado and bakes cookies, she'll die laughing. How quaint!"

When she was outside, Sara stopped to catch her breath and then hurried on, lest Louann decide to follow her and try to convince her she was Sara Carleton, after all.

As he had promised, Jackson waited at the entrance to the grandstand.

Sara ran and threw her arms around him. "Oh, Jackson, hold me!"

"Hey, hey, what's wrong?" He enfolded her in a

warm embrace. "You look as though you'd seen a ghost. You're not having a dizzy spell, are you? I thought those were all over."

"No, not a dizzy spell. I just wanted a hug."

"Anytime, honey, anytime." He chuckled and held her tighter.

His arms around her felt solid and safe. When Sara's heart slowed down and her breathing evened out, she eased herself from his arms. "Okay, I'm ready to see the show now."

"Let's go, then. Buck is really psyched. Molly and the guys are saving our seats."

As exciting as the rodeo show was, Sara's mind insisted on wandering back to the picture-taking session, to Louann's look of utter disbelief when Sara denied being Sara Carleton.

When Buck's turn came, and he and his horse burst from the chute, Sara managed to cheer with the others. She gripped Jackson's hand as the wild animal tossed Buck about. When the horse reared and he tumbled to the ground, she moaned with disappointment. She waited anxious moments, and then breathed with relief when Buck rose to his feet and, amid cheers from the crowd, stumbled off to the sidelines.

Later, on the way home, she laid her head against Jackson's shoulder. Not even his nearness could chase away her dread. Nor could his warm and loving kisses before they said goodnight.

"You okay?" Jackson brushed his lips across her forehead. "You seem preoccupied."

"I'm just tired."

"We have had a full day."

Sleep failed to provide the escape Sara hoped for. She dreamed about a woman who looked like Louann. "Bad Sara!" the dream-woman said, shaking a finger in her face. "I'm going to tell on you!"

****

"You saw Sara?" Grayson stared at Louann Brougham.

"It sure looked like her," Louann said with a nod.

"Tell me about it."

Grayson took Louann by the elbow and steered her to the edge of the crowd filling SoHo's Gilded Cage Gallery. The chic, but noisy, party was for an up-and-coming sculptor. Grayson had no particular interest in the man's work, but he always attended such occasions hoping to make connections to help his political career.

"I've been seeing Bret Hall, the photographer." Louann fluffed her blue-black hair. "He's having his own show next month, at the Sun and Moon Gallery. A very big show—"

"About Sara?" Grayson interrupted, barely keeping his tone civil. Louann could ramble on and on without ever getting to the point.

"Yes, well, he had an assignment from *Country View*, to do an article on county fairs throughout the west. I thought tagging along would be a novelty. He wouldn't need his cute little assistant if he had me, now, would he?" She gave him a saucy smile.

Keep to the point, Louann. "So you went on this trip and saw Sara?"

"Uh huh. In this funny little podunk town in Colorado. Out in the countryside. Do you know we had to drive more than an hour from Denver?"

Grayson had to grit his teeth to keep from nagging Louann to stay on track, but, finally, he learned the details of her "Sara sighting."

"And this person said she wasn't Sara?" he asked.

"She said her first name was Sara and that she lived there in Colorado. Then she hurried away to meet someone. I thought Sara was staying at one of

J. Edward's other homes. I've been told that whenever I've called her. But Sara's not one to go away without telling her friends."

Intuition told Grayson Louann had indeed seen the real Sara Carleton. He felt like doing a jig right there in the middle of the gallery, but, mindful of J. Edward's insistence on secrecy, he only said in a calm voice, "Oh, I don't know. Sara can be a very private person, sometimes. What did you say the name of the town was?"

Louann put a red-nailed finger to her cheek and tilted her head. "Glenn something. Glennriver? Glennstream? No, Glennbrook! That's it!"

"You're sure?" He leaned close, anxious for her answer.

"Yes, why?" Frowning, she studied him. "Grayson, is something going on here?"

He spread his hands. "No, no. I just wanted to be sure so I can tell Sara about her double. She'll find it amusing."

"Where is she, anyway?" Louann persisted.

Before he could form an answer, a woman sidled between them, rubbernecking to get a look at one of the sculptures. Grayson took the opportunity to step back and end the conversation with Louann.

"Got to move on. Talk to you later."

She fluttered her fingers. "Good seeing you. Tell Sara to call me when she gets home."

A few minutes later, Grayson left the gallery. The noise and the wine he'd drunk had started a headache. He took a taxi to Grand Central Station, arriving in time to catch the 10:15 train to Long Island. He settled into the seat and leaned back his head. When he reached home, he'd make plans to go to Glennbrook, Colorado. The trip might turn out to be a waste of time, but anything was better than sitting around waiting for news that never came.

****

"You're sure you don't want to come with me?" Jackson asked Sara. Today he planned to travel to Glennbrook, to see a lawyer Mike had recommended, who would advise them about how an amnesiac established a new identity.

Sara shook her head. "I promised Molly I'd spend the afternoon with her and the baby."

"But, you've known for a week I'd be going today." Would she really choose Molly and the baby over spending the day with him?

"You said you had business of your own to do there, too. I thought I'd be alone a lot of the time." She stood in the kitchen, her back to him, looking out the window.

Sensing something was wrong, he strode over and put his arms around her from behind, buried his face in her fragrant hair. Then he turned her around to face him. "Are you okay?"

"Sure." She kept her gaze averted.

"Sara, look at me." He cupped her chin and lifted her face.

"I'm fine," she insisted.

But her eyes looked bleak. "No, you're not. Ever since the fair, you've been different, somehow. I thought you were happy about what we decided."

"I am." She nodded.

"But you just haven't been...yourself."

A sad smile curved her lips. "Myself, that's a good one."

Refusing to share her weak attempt at humor, he kept his mouth tight. "The self I know, anyway. Sara. My Sara."

"Taking a new identity is a big step."

"I know, and I understand you might be frightened and uncertain." Jackson held her close, wanting to reassure her, wanting to infuse her with his strength. "But I love you so much, and I want us to be together."

Filled with emotion, he drew back and gazed into her eyes. He took her face in both his hands and kissed her. Her lips were warm and yielding, but when he pulled away, he saw her cheeks were wet with tears. One by one, he kissed them away.

"Everything will be all right," he told her. "I'll go to Glennbrook and see the lawyer, find out what needs to be done. You enjoy the afternoon with Molly and Karleen."

She reached out and touched his arm. "We'll have a nice dinner together when you come back."

****

Sara watched Jackson's truck head down the road to the highway. She wanted to accompany him, but was afraid she'd slip while at the lawyer's and give away her secret. Since running into Louann at the fair, she'd expected a call from Roger Decker at the police station, saying someone else had finally come looking for her. She knew Louann would tell Grayson and her father she'd seen Sara, or a woman who looked like her, and that would be all they needed to find her.

She must tell Jackson her memory had returned. As soon as he returned from Glennbrook, she'd confess. The time had come to bare her soul and take the consequences.

****

Later that afternoon, Jackson emerged from the lawyer's office into the bright sunshine. He'd found out all he needed to know about how Sara could legally establish herself as Sara. He wasn't as confident about the identity issue as he'd thought he would be, though. Something serious bothered her. He wished she'd confide in him. Was he a foolish dreamer to hope they could make their relationship permanent?

Be positive. She loves you. She's told you often enough.

Jackson decided to grab a bite to eat before heading back to Red Rock. Familiar with Glennbrook's restaurants, he sought out Jessup's on Main Street. He sat at the counter rather than in the dining room, hoping service would be quicker there. He wanted to eat and be on his way. Although he'd been gone only a few hours, already he missed Sara and was eager to return. He always missed her when they were apart.

He ordered a French dip sandwich and coffee, and then glanced around the room. There weren't many customers. The only other person at the counter was a man of about his age, sitting at the other end. The guy's gray slacks, black windbreaker, and styled hair said Big City. He was showing something to the waitress. Deciding the man was a salesman, Jackson dismissed him from his thoughts.

A few minutes later, the stranger slipped onto the stool beside his.

"Excuse me. May I have a minute of your time?"

Definitely an outsider. No one around here talked with such formality. "Depends," Jackson replied. Instinct told him to be wary.

The stranger ignored Jackson's cool response. "I'm Grayson Delacourt, from New York. I'm looking for this woman." He pulled several snapshots from his inside jacket pocket and spread them on the counter.

Jackson looked at the photos with only mild interest, and then did a double take.

Except for dark mascara and bright lipstick, the woman looked exactly like Sara. His Sara.

His heart began to jackhammer. No, it couldn't be her. He looked again. Yes, there were the big blue eyes, the pert nose, the oh-so-kissable mouth.

"Have you seen her?" Grayson Delacourt asked.

Jackson took a split second to compose himself. He mustn't let this man see any inkling of recognition on his face until he knew more about this. "I don't know. She looks like a lot of women I've seen. Who is she?"

"Her name is Sara Carleton. She's twenty-two years old and lives on Long Island, New York. Her father is J. Edward Carleton, the Third."

Jackson's insides took another jolt. Carleton was a well-known real estate developer and a big investor on Wall Street.

This time, he hadn't covered up his response, for Grayson said, "You look like you've heard of him."

He dropped his chin in a nod. "I used to work on Wall Street."

"No kidding? For whom?"

"Dalthorp and James, but tell me more about her." Jackson pointed to the photos.

"She disappeared almost three months ago."

"Didn't her father report her missing to the police?"

"No. He doesn't want any publicity. They had an argument and she took off. The next day she called to tell him she was all right." He shrugged. "That's the last we've heard from her."

"What was the argument about?"

"I don't know. J. Edward never told me. A couple of weeks later, some of her credit card charges came in from Denver. J. Edward still wouldn't go to the police. I hired a private detective, but he hasn't turned up anything."

Jackson shifted his gaze to the photos again, hoping he'd see them differently than before. No such luck. The woman still looked like his Sara. "So what brought you here?" he asked.

"Last week, a friend of ours saw a woman she thought was Sara at the county fair here in Glennbrook. The woman had won a prize in a baking contest. She said her name was Sara, and that she lived in Colorado. My friend said she acted strangely, though. I decided to come here and see if I could find this Sara. It's the only lead I have." He reached up to smooth his sandy-brown hair.

The waitress set Jackson's food in front of him. He stared at the steaming sandwich, but his appetite was gone, his stomach now in a knot. "What's your interest in this?"

"Sara and I are engaged to be married."

Grayson's words hit Jackson like a blow to the gut. Yet, he had to make sure he'd heard correctly. "You and this Sara were going to be married?"

"Are going to be," Grayson corrected. "The date's only a couple of months away."

He wanted to tell Grayson there would be no wedding, even if Sara were found, because she belonged to him now. He took a deep breath instead, and went on with his charade. "What do you think happened to her?"

Grayson shrugged. "She must have had an accident and lost her memory. I know she wouldn't stay away this long, otherwise. But, hey, I don't want to keep you from your lunch. If you see her, I'd appreciate a call." He gave Jackson a business card then scooped up the photos.

As Grayson slid off the stool, Jackson asked, "Are you contacting the police while you're here?"

Grayson shook his head. "J. Edward would have a fit if I did."

"He sounds like quite a guy."

"Very stubborn, to say the least. I do plan to hunt up the people who put on the contest at the fair, though. I'm sure to get some information from them. Thanks for your time."

"No problem." Jackson watched Grayson return to his original seat. He picked up his sandwich and took a bite, but the food stuck in his throat. He couldn't eat and he couldn't stand being in the same room with Grayson Delacourt. He called to the waitress for his check.

Outside, Jackson headed for his truck, his mind whirling with what he'd learned from Grayson Delacourt. The incident at the fair might explain why Sara had been troubled since then. But, why hadn't she told him about the woman who'd thought she was Sara Carleton?

Maybe she didn't want to upset him. Maybe she'd brushed it off as a mistake, like that guy, Howard, had made in thinking Sara was his wife. There could be many reasons why she hadn't mentioned the occurrence.

More important, she was about to be found. When Delacourt located the fair officials, they would lead him to the Rolling R. He'd claim Sara and take her back to New York. The thought of losing her sent Jackson into a tailspin. He couldn't allow it. Not now, not when they'd fallen in love and were ready to spend the rest of their lives together.

A wild and crazy plan sprouted in his mind. Instead of continuing on to his truck, he headed for the nearest phone booth. Grabbing the phone book, he turned to the Yellow Pages. Aha, the establishment he sought was located only two blocks away. He hurried toward it.

Half an hour later, Jackson emerged from the building full of excitement and anticipation. He climbed into his truck and began the journey home. He could hardly wait to tell Sara about his surprise. Good thing he was only half an hour away.

However, the trip home was long enough for some of his euphoria to wear off and doubts to creep in. Did he have the right to control Sara's life? Did he have the right to withhold the truth?

But she loved him. Nothing else mattered.

Hadn't she loved Grayson, though? Why else would she become engaged to him?

On the other hand, Sara was happy with her

new life. Why make her miserable by exposing her to the old one? There must have been something she didn't like about her past or she wouldn't have run away.

His mind still churning, Jackson pulled his truck into the garage at the Rolling R. He turned off the engine and sat there, planning what he would say when he walked into the house and faced Sara.

Taking a deep breath, he leaped from the truck. He strode straight and tall to the back door of the house, where he stopped, took another deep breath, and then opened the screen door and stepped inside.

He expected to find Sara in the kitchen, where she usually hung out, experimenting with new recipes.

The kitchen was empty. Eerily empty. Apprehension skittered down his spine as he walked deeper into the house.

He found her in the living room. She stood at the window with her back to him. Just the sight of her made him realize he couldn't go through with his crazy scheme. He couldn't live with himself if he was deceitful. He'd have to tell her the truth and trust she loved him enough to choose him and their new life over Grayson and her old one.

"Hey, Sara, I'm home."

Keeping her gaze focused out the window, she nodded. "I saw your truck."

Her voice sounded strained. He took a step toward her just as she turned around. When he saw her eyes, puffy and red-rimmed from crying, an ominous chill gripped him.

"Sara, what's wrong?"

"I - I have something to tell you."

"What?"

"I know who I am."

Chapter Fourteen

Sara watched the blood drain from Jackson's face. She'd hoped he'd take her into his arms, but they hung limply at his side. "I'm sorry," she rushed on. "I didn't mean to be so blunt. While I waited for you to return, I've been trying to decide just how I should break the news, and when I saw you, my words tumbled out."

"Who are you, then?" he asked.

"My name is Sara Carleton. I live on Long Island, New York."

"I know."

She gasped. Of all the reactions she'd expected, that wasn't one. "You know? How?"

"I found out today, in Glennbrook. I was in Jessup's restaurant and a man came over to me. Said his name was Grayson Delacourt. He had photos of you and asked me if I knew you."

Alarm arrowed through her, and she hugged her arms. "Grayson? In Glennbrook?"

"Yes, he said he was your fiancé. Is that true?"

With all her heart, she wished it wasn't. She swallowed hard. "Yes."

"He said a friend of yours from New York recognized you at the fair."

As she'd feared, Louann had given her away. She nodded. "Louann Brougham. But, did you tell Grayson you knew me and where I was living?"

"No. I didn't want him to find you. I had this crazy plan. I went to a travel agency and bought tickets for a cruise." He took the tickets from his shirt pocket and tossed them on the coffee table.

"Then, when I came in just now, I knew I couldn't go through with such a lie."

Sara stared at the tickets, touched by his last-ditch effort to keep the two of them together.

"So what exactly have you remembered besides your name?" he asked.

Realizing her knees were a bit wobbly, she sank into a nearby chair. "I had an argument with my father and decided to take a train trip across the country. I was headed for California."

"Really? What were you trying to prove?"

She shrugged. "A way of asserting my independence, I guess. My father is very controlling. He's always making decisions for me. I wanted to run my own life, for a change."

"What was the argument about?"

"About my marrying Grayson. My father wanted me to, but I didn't. I did accept Grayson's ring, but then I panicked and told Dad I couldn't marry him after all. He wouldn't accept my change of heart." Holding a breath, she glanced his way to see his reaction so far.

Jackson turned away and strode to the window, keeping his back to her. "Why did he choose Grayson?"

"I don't know. My father likes him, thinks he'd be good for me."

"What about your mother?"

"She died when I was three." Even now, the words were hard to say. "Except for my grandmother and a series of nannies, I was pretty much raised by my father." Sara relaxed a little. So far, he seemed to accept what she told him without becoming angry, as she'd feared. But his back was still to her, and she couldn't see his expression.

The room was silent, except for the ticking of the clock on the fireplace mantel. She wished he'd say something. What was he thinking?

She was just about to ask him if he were okay when he wheeled around and faced her. He stuck his hands on his hips and narrowed his eyes. Uh oh, not good.

"Exactly when did you remember all this?" he demanded.

With all her heart, Sara wanted to say, "Today." But she knew she must tell the truth. No more lies. Lies didn't solve anything; they only led to more trouble.

Still, her chest ached and the words stuck in her throat. "My, ah, memory came back the...the day you picked me up from the hospital."

"You're kidding me, right?"

"No, I'm not kidding. I wish I were."

He took a few steps toward her. "You mean to tell me, all the time you've been staying here, you've been pretending to have a loss of memory?

His harsh tone made her cringe inside. She crossed her arms over her chest. "That's right."

Jackson's face turned red.

"I'm really sorry—" Tears burned her eyes.

"Sorry?" he exploded. "You used me. And Rose. And everyone here. You played on our sympathy, our wanting to help you, when all the time you could've returned home and faced your father."

Sara held out her hands, palms up. "But I just told you he's very controlling. I wanted to get away from him."

"You can't run away from your problems, Sara. Don't you know that?"

"I thought I could..."

"What do you think now?"

She dropped her hands back into her lap and lowered her gaze. "I know you're right. But, Jackson, I never meant to hurt you. Or Rose. Or anyone. I was trying to buy myself some time until I could decide what to do. Until I had some money of my own. So, when you offered me a job, I took it."

"I feel like such a fool," Jackson said. "The hypnotist, the lawyer I saw today, all my worrying about you. All a waste of time."

"I'm truly sorry," she said again. If only he would understand.

"And your so-called love for me? Hah. Just a sham to keep in my good graces while you saved up the money to leave."

"No! My feelings are real!"

"Real? You expect me to believe you?" He shook his head. "I don't think so."

She bent her head and hugged her arms. His disbelief in her love was a deep blow.

"Didn't you think the truth would come out sometime?" he went on.

"Yes, I kept thinking I should tell you. But I couldn't bring myself to do it. I was afraid you wouldn't understand."

He nodded. "You were right. What you've done is beyond my understanding. Well, Grayson is on your trail now. He's contacting the folks who put on the contest at the fair." He waved a hand. "That'll be a fun scene, won't it, when he comes knocking on my door?"

Sara's worst fears about confessing had come true. Jackson hated her. And no, she didn't want Grayson to come here. She wouldn't subject either herself or Jackson to that.

Which brought her to another decision. Good thing she'd had an alternate plan in the back of her mind. "He won't come here."

"Of course, he will. He'll find out where you are from the fair officials."

She lifted her chin. "I'll call him on his cell and tell him I'm returning to Long Island. I'm catching the seven o'clock train."

His eyes widened. "Tonight?"

Sara nodded, dread churning her stomach.

"So you're going back and what? Stand up to your father, after all? Or marry Grayson, like he wants you to?"

Sara looked away. "I don't know what will happen when I get home."

"Well, fine. I guess I'm driving you into Red Rock, then."

"No. Buck said to give him a call, if I needed a ride."

"So, this is good-bye."

It was a statement, not a question. Her heart sank. She'd held out the hope he would understand. She wanted him to forgive her and wait while she went home and straightened out her old life. But the opposite had happened. Yet, could she blame him? Wouldn't she feel the same way if their situations were reversed?

"Yes, it is," she replied. "But I want to thank you for all your help—"

He waved a hand. "Oh, spare me. Just forget it, will you? I'd like to forget this whole thing ever happened." He crossed his arms over his chest and turned his back again.

So, this was the end, then. Shaken, Sara struggled to her feet. For a second, her legs were so wobbly she thought she would fall when she tried to walk. Summoning all her remaining strength, she managed to take a couple steps forward.

"I found a small suitcase in the upstairs closet," she said before leaving the room. "I hope you don't mind if I borrow it. I'll send it back when I get—" She stopped. She'd almost said, "home." But Long Island wasn't home, not anymore.

Yet, after today, neither was the Rolling R. Like an orphan, she was about to be cast adrift.

"You can keep it, for all I care," was Jackson's terse reply.

"Thanks... Your supper's in the oven."

"I'm not hungry," he growled.

Tears burning her eyes, Sara crept upstairs to pack.

****

As soon as Sara was out of sight, Jackson marched into the kitchen. Not even the aromas of pork chops and applesauce tempted him to stop. He continued out the back door and to the barn. Like a robot, he went about his chores.

Yet, he couldn't put aside the scene he'd just had with Sara, nor could he come to grips with the outcome. This morning, he'd kissed her good-bye and set out for Glennbrook, full of hope for their future. Now, just hours later, that future had burned to ashes.

He'd come home to find a stranger. A stranger who had lied and taken advantage of him.

A stranger he'd fallen in love with.

Well, the love was over. All washed up. How could he love someone who'd deceived him? He didn't care what the reason was. As far as he was concerned, she should have been truthful about the recovery of her memory. He wished he'd never locked gazes with her in the train station in the first place, or discovered her in the alley.

A truck rumbling down the road caught his attention. Probably Buck, coming to pick up Sara. He went to the door, looked out, and recognized Buck's pickup.

Glad for his foreman's help, he shut the door and continued checking on the horses. Jenny and her new foal were next. Sara had named the foal Amber, because of its mellow, golden color. He reached in the stall and patted Amber's sleek nose.

"She's leaving us," he whispered.

A shadow fell across the cement floor. Jackson looked up to see Buck. His expression was grim.

"Came to take Sara to the train," he said.

"So I heard." Jackson gave Amber another pat.

"I just wanted to make sure what I'm doin' is all right with you," Buck said.

"Sure is. Saves me the trouble." Jackson knew his tone was terse but hoped Buck would understand the stress he was under.

Buck opened his mouth, as though he wanted to say more, but Jackson turned away, indicating the conversation was over. He heard the barn door close as Buck left.

A few minutes later, his truck roared to life. The sound of it traveling down the road took forever to fade away.

****

Sara opened her eyes and blinked at her surroundings. This was not her cozy bedroom at the Rolling R, but her spacious bedroom on Long Island. Her gaze roved past the carved bedposts of her king-size, canopied bed to the mammoth armoire against one wall.

Only last year, she'd chosen the furnishings, thinking them glamorous and elegant. Now, compared to her plain, yet comfortable room at the ranch, this decor struck her as gaudy and overdone.

With a moan, she turned over and buried her head under the pillow. What a letdown. After a few months of glorious freedom, she'd returned to prison. She lay there awhile, peeking now and then at the bedside clock. In the Carleton household, breakfast was served promptly at eight o'clock. She had a mind to ignore that and stay in bed longer.

However, this was her first morning back. She'd yet to decide her future course of action. For now, she'd follow her father's schedule.

Half an hour later, Sara descended the marble staircase to the first floor. She followed the hallway to the dining room, where August sunlight beamed through the tall, narrow windows, casting elongated shadows over the high-ceilinged room. The fragrance of chrysanthemums from the huge bouquet on the mahogany sideboard filled the air.

Her father sat at one end of the table, perusing the morning newspaper. He looked up and they exchanged perfunctory "Good mornings," and then she took her usual place at the opposite end of the table.

Sophie, the cook, entered and delivered Sara's usual breakfast of scrambled eggs and toast. Sara sighed. She'd fallen back into the routine as though she'd never left.

After awhile her father put down his newspaper and said, "Well, Sara, I could scold you for your stupid actions, but I don't want to waste the time. You're back now, and we can get on with our lives."

"What did you tell people about my absence?" Sara asked, as she picked at her food. Being home and around her father again had taken away her appetite.

"That you've been staying at our other homes."

"What about Louann's seeing me at the fair?"

"A simple case of mistaken identity." He wrinkled his nose. "Entering cookies at a county fair! What were you thinking?"

Sara gritted her teeth. "You know I've always liked to cook."

"But Sara Carleton winning a prize at a county fair? We can't let that get out." He waved a hand. "It's all best forgotten now."

She'd been trying to forget, but hadn't yet succeeded. Memories of Jackson and of her life on the ranch kept popping up.

Her father picked up a small silver bell near his plate and rang it.

Sophie bustled in.

"I'll have my coffee now." He looked at Sara.

"How about you?"

"I guess so," she replied, although nothing appealed to her this morning.

His frowning gaze zeroed in on her plate. "You'd better eat up. Grayson will be here soon." He leaned forward to peer at her. "You're going to be married in a couple of months. He has a brilliant political future."

"So you keep telling me."

"Well, it's true. He's getting ready to run for the state's House of Representatives. This campaign is only the start of what I predict will be a stunning political career. You'll be a great asset to him."

Sara bristled. He'd never asked her if she wanted to be in the pubic eye. As usual, he just assumed she would go along with his and Grayson's plans.

Sophie returned with a silver carafe and poured their coffee. She set the carafe on the table and clasped her hands across her ample stomach. "Will that be all, Mr. Edward?"

"Yes, Sophie, thank you."

As Sara's father sipped his brew, he looked at her over the rim of his cup. Folds of skin wrinkled his high forehead. "Sara, this Jackson fellow. You and he didn't ...ah, what I mean is—"

"If you're asking if we had an affair, the answer is no, we didn't."

His brow smoothed and a satisfied smile curved his thin lips. "At least, you did something right."

Indignation heated her cheeks. "Jackson and his sister took me in when I had no money or credit cards and no place to go. Which reminds me, did any credit card bills come in?"

"Yes, but only a few. We believed you'd made the charges, although some of the purchases didn't seem like things you'd buy. I paid them, anyway, and there weren't any more after that. Who knows why?

Maybe the thieves were arrested for something else and unable to use the cards anymore. I'll have my secretary cancel them and get you some new ones."

"No, Dad. I'll do it. I need to start doing things for myself."

J. Edward's eyebrows shot up. "Getting awfully independent, aren't you?"

"It's about time, wouldn't you say? Anyway, I'm very thankful to Jackson and Rose for rescuing me."

"Hmmm. Perhaps I should send them some compensation."

Sara stiffened. "Please don't. Jackson would be insulted."

"And what was his reaction when he found out you'd deceived him with a phony memory loss?"

"He, ah, wasn't too happy," Sara admitted, cringing inwardly at the memory.

J. Edward snorted. "I don't blame him. I hope you've learned a lesson."

Not knowing how to reply, Sara stared at her plate.

Her father went on, "Well, as I said, the whole fiasco is best forgotten."

****

Sitting in his favorite leather recliner, his feet propped up on a footstool, his stomach full of Anna's savory pot roast, Jackson still couldn't relax.

After Sara had left, he'd hoped to restore harmony to his life, but he couldn't stop thinking about her and the traumatic end to their relationship. She was gone. He wished he could make the pain go away as well, but his heart continued to ache with loss and loneliness.

The phone rang. He considered not answering. He always wished Sara were on the other end of the line, and was always disappointed when she wasn't.

However, not answering wasn't an option. He had a business to run, and calls could be important.

Linda Hope Lee

Hope rose as he snatched up the receiver, then, at the caller's deep male voice, turned to disappointment.

"This is Ralph Epson. Is Sara there?"

Expecting the call to be for him, Jackson swallowed his surprise. "Why, no. Can I ask why you're calling her?"

"Sure. I'm with the Golden Baking Company. You've heard of us?"

"Can't say I have." Jackson grew more curious. What was this all about?

"We make all your popular baked goods. Pies, cakes, cookies."

"Okay, but why are you calling Sara?"

"One of our scouts was at your county fair a couple of weeks ago. We're interested in adding Sara's Peppermint Dreams to our cookie line."

"No kidding?"

Before Jackson could explain that Sara's absence was permanent, rather than temporary, Ralph Epson went on, "I'll give you my phone number. Have her call me when she comes in. I'm in the area for the next few days and would like to set up a meeting."

"I'll give her the message. But she might not get back to you in time to get together while you're here."

"Then we'll arrange something else."

Jackson grabbed a pencil and wrote down the man's number. After he hung up, he wondered about what he was doing. Why hadn't he told Epson to look up the Carletons's number in New York instead of taking on the burden himself? Now, he'd have to phone the Carleton home and relay the message.

He doubted Sara would be interested in Epson's proposition. She'd be absorbed in her wedding plans. Besides, she didn't need the money such an offer would bring. Her father was loaded.

150

Still, he either must pass on the message, or call Epson back and let him track Sara down in New York. Jackson drummed his fingers on the chair arm, trying to decide what to do. Finally, he folded the slip of paper and put it in his shirt pocket.

****

"Running away was stupid," Grayson said. "I still have trouble believing you would do something so inconsiderate to me and your father."

"I didn't think my action was stupid at the time," Sara said, tired of defending her actions. "And I still don't."

A week had passed since Sara had retuned to Long Island, and she and Grayson sat on a brocaded settee in the Carleton's living room. She took a moment to study him. While she'd been away, she'd all but forgotten what he looked like. His features were pleasant enough, and his hair, combed straight back from his high forehead, was a nice sandy-brown. His blue eyes radiated intelligence.

Still, he fell sadly short when compared to Jackson Phillips.

Forget about Jackson Phillips.

Her heart ached and she wished she could.

"What got into you, Sara? Help me to understand."

"I just had to get away for a while. I feel so...so stifled here."

Grayson frowned. "Why? You have everything you could possibly want. We'll have a wonderful life after we're married."

Sara bit her lip. Her marriage to Grayson was the reason she'd left. "Grayson, about that..."

Her father stuck his head in the door. "Here you two are. Been looking all over for you." He glanced from one to the other. "Everything okay?"

"Just fine," Grayson said.

"Dad, Grayson and I have to talk. Then I'll need

151

to talk to you."

He frowned. "Later, Sara. Grayson and I need to have our own discussion. In my office, Gray. Now."

"Yes, sir." Grayson jumped up then turned to Sara. "Go, uh, fix your hair or something. Whatever you girls do. I'll be back soon."

After they left, Sara harrumphed and crossed her arms over her chest. Fix her hair indeed. She hated being talked down to. She hadn't realized how annoying and insulting his manner was, until she'd spent time away from home.

Jackson would never be condescending. Sara sighed. No use thinking about him anymore. He hated her. She regretted deceiving him, but at the time, she'd been desperate. In her mind, she'd had no other choice. She wished he would have understood.

But he hadn't.

And now she would never see him again. Sadness filled her.

Well, just because she would never be with Jackson again didn't mean she had to marry Grayson, either. She'd been about to tell him when her father interrupted them.

She twisted her hands in her lap, thinking about her father and his insistence on choosing Grayson as her husband. Why him? Why couldn't she marry a man of her own choosing?

One thing was certain—she was through taking orders from her father. She would stand up for herself. First would be her refusal to marry Grayson. She'd be firm. No giving in.

She might as well tell both of them at the same time. She rose from the couch. Why not now?

Leaving the living room, she marched down the hallway to her father's office. The door was ajar. Her father's and Grayson's voices came from inside the room. Good, they were still having their meeting.

She was about to enter the room when she heard Grayson say something about "Sara's trust fund."

"Don't worry about that," her father said. "As soon as she has her birthday, we'll put our plan in the works."

Trust fund? A chill ran over her skin. What were they talking about? Instead of interrupting them, as she'd planned, she stopped to listen.

"I hope we can get control of the money without too much trouble," Grayson said. "Two million is a big chunk of change."

Two million? Sara's jaw dropped.

"I sure need that money to jumpstart my campaign," Grayson went on.

"A campaign you'd better win," her father said. A hollow thump against wood sounded. "We developers in this state need more legislators on our side. Far too often, the environmentalists get the upper hand. The site I've been wanting to develop in Eastgate has been tied up for years."

"I'll do my best," Grayson said. After a pause, he continued, "Sara seems different since she's come back. She's not the Sara I knew before. "

"We'll be able to handle her. She always does what I tell her to."

Sara struggled to make sense of what she heard. Her stomach drew into a tight knot as the men spoke. Apparently, she was to come into a sizable trust fund on her next birthday, which was in a few months. She had never been told of this.

More important, her father and Grayson planned to use the money for Grayson's political campaign.

How dare they! Sara balled her hands into fists. All thoughts of being kind and apologetic about her decision not to marry Grayson fled. Of course, she would not marry him. Never in a million years.

Sara pushed the door farther open and burst

into the room. "What's this about a trust fund?"

The men turned to her, eyes wide.

"You were eavesdropping?" her father said. "Really, Sara, where are your manners?"

Sara crossed her arms over her chest and thrust out her chin. "Never mind. I want to know about the trust fund."

Her father cleared his throat. "Yes, well, your Grandmother Millie left it to you."

Dear Grandmother Millie, the woman who'd helped to raise her. "Why was I never told?"

"Your mother wanted to surprise you."

"With a lot of prodding from you, I bet." She shifted her attention to Grayson. "I heard you say you want the money for your campaign."

He briefly met her gaze, and then looked away.

"The money will be well spent." Her father stood and took a step toward her. "For your future."

"What do you mean?" she asked.

"Once Grayson gets elected, he—and the others my cohorts and I have managed to put in office—will work to get legislation passed that is favorable to developers. I'll be able to continue my work. The more work I do, the more money I make. When I die, everything goes to you, Sara." He gestured toward the windows facing the courtyard. "You're my only heir."

"Why not use some of the money you already have for Grayson?"

"Because all my liquid assets are tied up right now."

Inside, she fumed. "Well, you can't have my money."

"But when you and Grayson are married—"

"No." She held up her hand to stop him. "We're not getting married. That's what I came to tell you."

Grayson finally came to life and jumped to his feet. "You had something going with that guy in

Colorado, didn't you? I knew your relationship with him wasn't so innocent."

Her father waved a hand in Grayson's direction. "Shut up, Gray! Let me handle this." In a calmer tone, he said to Sara, "You're not yourself yet. Why don't you go upstairs and rest awhile? I'll have Sophie bring up some tea."

"Yes, I'll go upstairs," Sara said, biting out each word. "But not to rest. To pack a few things and leave. This time, I won't be back."

He shook a finger at her. "Sara, I forbid you to leave this house!"

"You can't hold me prisoner. I'm a free person. Freer than I've ever been."

"Your credit cards will take you only so far."

"You're forgetting that in a few months I'll have a big chunk of change, as Grayson put it. I have enough cash and jewelry I can sell to last until then. And in case you have any thoughts about getting hold of the fund beforehand, forget it. I'm putting in a call right now to our lawyer."

Her father's eyes blazed. "After all I've done for you, I can't believe you'd act this way."

A rush of insight flooded Sara, tugging at her chest. "All you've done for me has really been for yourself. You've never cared in the least what I might want." She turned on her heel and headed for the door.

"You'll be sorry!" her father called after her.

Chapter Fifteen

Upstairs in her room, Sara marched to her walk-in closet and flung open the doors. Since she'd already returned Jackson's suitcase, she took out another, larger one. The first time, she'd run away with only the clothes on her back. This time, she'd take more. But not too much. She wanted to cut as many ties to this life as she could.

She opened a dresser drawer, grabbed some underwear, and tossed it into the case. Her hands shook so badly she finally gave up and sank onto the bed. Taking deep breaths, she wrapped her arms around her waist and rocked back and forth. How could her father do such a horrible thing and then say he had only her best interest at heart?

She wished she'd never returned to Long Island.

Then a thought struck. If she hadn't come back, she'd never have discovered her father's and Grayson's scheme. A painful lesson, but one she needed to learn.

Okay, but where would she go now?

Returning to the Rolling R was out of the question. Her deception had hurt Jackson. His hurt had turned to anger and, ultimately, to rejection.

No, she could not go back to him.

She thought of the other time she'd run away. She'd planned to travel across the country to California. But, because of what had happened in Red Rock, she'd never reached her destination. Why not begin the journey again and complete it this time? The West Coast was far from her father and Grayson. There she'd be free to make a life for herself. Perhaps she'd find a job as a chef. Doing what she loved to do.

Sara took a deep breath and squared her shoulders. She could finish her packing now. First, though, she'd call her lawyer and secure her trust fund.

****

"Seems kinda silly to take you only to the train station," Buck told Jackson, "when I should drive you all the way to the airport in Denver."

Jackson stashed his bag behind the front seat of Buck's truck and climbed in. "I know, but I'm planning to visit Rose before my plane leaves."

"Okay, you're the boss." Buck stationed himself behind the steering wheel, started the engine, and they were on their way.

Visiting Rose was only one reason Jackson wanted to take the train to Denver. But, even though Buck was a good friend, Jackson didn't want to admit he had the crazy urge to be in the Red Rock station again, where he'd first seen Sara. He wasn't sure why that was important. It just was.

The other part of the plan was to visit her Long Island home, using the message from the Golden Baking Company as his excuse. At first, he'd thought seeing her again in her old environment would help to purge her from his system. Then he decided he was only kidding himself. He still loved Sara, despite her deception. Since he'd had time to think about it, he understood why she'd chosen to keep her memory recovery a secret. He regretted his anger and the unhappy scene they'd had.

He would declare his love for her and hope she still felt the same way about him. If she didn't, he would accept her decision, no matter how painful. His hand clenched on the truck's armrest. At least, he'd have closure.

"You say you'll be gone about a week?" Buck's

voice broke into his thoughts.

"Yeah. A week should give me enough time."

Jackson had told Buck and Molly he was going to New York to look up old friends, which he intended to do. If they suspected his trip had something to do with Sara, they were keeping it to themselves.

"Karli's christening's on the twenty-fifth," Buck reminded him when they'd left the Rolling R and were on the highway.

"I'll be back in time. Don't worry."

"We couldn't christen her without her godfather bein' there." Buck grinned sideways at him.

"I know, and, believe me, I won't miss it."

Buck slowed as they came up behind a truckload of hay. "We still haven't decided who's to be her godmother. We was kinda hopin' it would be Sara."

Buck's words echoed his own thoughts. "You know that's out of the question now."

"Right."

"Say, don't forget to check on the irrigation lines in the upper pasture. Since a pipe was plugged before, we want to keep an eye on it."

"Got it on my list."

The hay truck switched to the exit lane, and Buck stepped on the gas.

Jackson made sure he filled the remainder of the ride with talk about what Buck and the others needed to do while he was gone.

At last, the train station came into sight. Buck pulled to a stop in the loading zone.

Jackson hopped out, and then grabbed his bag from behind the seat. "Thanks for the ride, buddy. See you soon."

"Take care." Buck waved and then he sped away.

Bag slung over his shoulder, Jackson studied the old brick building. Did he really want to go inside? Yeah, he did. Lifting his chin, he strode toward the station's entrance.

****

Only half-awake but aware the train had slowed, Sara shifted in her seat. The swaying motion had lulled her to sleep. She didn't mind, though, for today they were traveling through Colorado, and missing that part of the trip would be for the best.

The train continued to decrease speed. Several passengers moved past her and on down the aisle. Behind them came a conductor, wearing his uniform of black pants and tan jacket with the train logo printed in red on the pocket.

Just then, the train lurched to a stop.

"Where are we?" Sara asked him.

"Red Rock, ma'am."

Sara's mouth went dry. "We're not stopping here, are we? I didn't see it on the schedule."

"We are stopping. Guess you didn't read the schedule right. We have a half-hour layover, plenty of time to get off and stretch your legs." A passenger up ahead beckoned and he moved on.

Sara regarded Red Rock's brick station though the window. Why would she want to be here again? This was where the awful attack had taken place.

This was where she'd met Jackson.

Thinking of their last time together brought a sudden lump to her throat. She'd handled their parting as best she could, but the heartache it left behind had yet to heal.

A sudden urge to get off the train and enter the station gripped her. She told herself being there again might help her to recall some new details about the attack that would help the police. Although the police were no longer actively investigating her case, Sergeant Decker had said to be sure to notify him if she remembered anything new.

She'd called him from Long Island to apologize about her deception. Instead of being angry, as Jackson had, Decker had said he understood and wished her luck. Sara sighed. She wished Jackson could've been like the police officer. But, then, Decker hadn't been in love with her, either. Jackson's love was based on high expectations. She'd learned that the hard way.

Sara left her seat and walked down the aisle to the exit. After a moment's hesitation, she stepped down onto the pavement. A rush of warm, dry Colorado air washed over her. Several people passed by on their way to the stationhouse. She focused on remembering the other time she'd been there, hoping to recall something new to help the police find her assailants.

Hoping to avoid thinking of Jackson.

She entered the station and spotted the bench where she'd sat to call her father. She'd had to wait while Foster summoned him to the phone. While she waited, she'd idly looked around...and seen a cowboy reading a newspaper at the newsstand.

A cowboy who turned out to be Jackson Phillips.

She recalled in vivid detail how their gazes had met across the room and held for what seemed like forever. She'd thought him the most handsome man she'd ever seen. Her heartbeat quickened at the memory.

More than eye contact had taken place, she now realized. Unbelievable as it was, a strong, deep connection had been made in those few moments. In that brief time, she had fallen in love with him.

Sara's mind spun a fantastic scenario. What if she had been destined to be in this place, at exactly that time, so she could meet Jackson, her true love? Fate had again intervened when she'd been attacked and lost her memory. Jackson and Rose had rescued her, so she and Jackson could be together and begin a relationship.

All well and good, but then her memory had returned, and she'd begun to weave her web of deceit. A web that in the end destroyed their relationship and his love.

A deep sense of loss consumed Sara. How stupid she'd been. If only she'd made different choices.

She looked at the newsstand again...and did a double take. Her breath caught in her throat.

A man stood reading a newspaper in the same exact place Jackson had that fateful day. This man's build was similar to his—tall and muscular with a broad chest tapering to narrow hips. He wore a tan cowboy hat, just like one Jackson had.

But, of course, this man wasn't Jackson. No way.

The man turned in her direction and she glimpsed his face underneath the brim of the cowboy hat. Square jaw, expressive mouth, and the tip of a bold nose. Her heart skipped a beat. He certainly looked like Jackson.

No, she was seeing only what she so desperately wanted to see. Wishful thinking caused her to hallucinate.

The man raised his head. His gaze roamed the station, and then landed on her. His eyes widened in shock and disbelief.

Jackson! Sara's pulse pounded. She wanted to run to him, but, remembering their angry parting, kept her feet rooted in place.

Jackson wasn't of the same mind. Long-legged strides sped him to her side. "Sara, is that you?" He looked at her with wide eyes.

His nearness took her breath away. She paused long enough to take in the features of his beloved face. "Y-yes, it's me."

"What are you doing here?"

Sara swallowed hard and managed to answer

his question. "I'm taking the train trip across the country that I started before. I didn't know the train stopped here. But when it did, I got off to see—"

Oh, oh, careful here. Don't let him know he had anything to do with your decision.

She lifted her chin and finished, "To see if I could remember anything more about the attack to tell the police."

"Really?"

He kept his gaze glued to hers. Could he tell she'd told only part of the truth? Heat suffused her, along with the sudden urge to blurt out all her feelings, lay herself bare. She said instead, "Where are you going? Or are you returning from somewhere?"

"I'm on my way to New York."

She gasped and stepped back. "New York?"

"To see you."

Her mouth went dry. "What do you mean?"

"We can't talk here in the middle of the station. Let's sit." He nodded to the rows of benches.

"But the train—"

"Is the same one I'm taking. I won't let you miss it."

When they both were seated, he began, "I was going New York to deliver a message to you from someone. I'll tell you later what it is." He paused, as though considering what to say next. "Okay, I'll be truthful, Sara. The message also was my excuse to see you again."

"But why?"

"I didn't like the way we parted. I lost my head and got angry."

His confession gave her courage to respond in kind. Her throat scratched but she forced out her words. "And I hurt you. I never meant to."

He nodded. "Neither of us handled it well, did we? At first, I thought if I could see you one last time in your former life, then I'd have closure to what happened between us."

She bit her lip and looked away, and then said in a flat voice, "I see."

"Wait, Sara." He reached out and took her hand. "That's what I told myself. But that wasn't true. The truth is, I still love you. I decided to find you and fight for you."

Furrowing her brows, unable to believe what she'd just heard, she returned her gaze to him. "You still love me?"

"I do. More than ever."

Sara felt lightheaded, as though she might faint. "I love you, too," she whispered.

A slow smile curved his lips. "I was hoping to hear those words."

His comment gave her courage to reveal more of her feelings. "When I came in the station just now, I remembered the first time we saw each other, how our gazes met and something special passed between us. I realized I fell in love with you in that moment. I know it sounds crazy, but it's true."

He pushed a lock of hair back from her face, letting his fingers linger on her cheek. "The same thing happened to me, but I'd convinced myself I wasn't ready for someone new. But what about now? Have we lost everything? I thought when you left our relationship was over."

"No, no, my love for you didn't get lost. I had to put it on hold while I took care of unfinished business in New York. I never loved Grayson. Please believe me. Like I told you, my father insisted I marry him. But I've told them both I never will. Now, I'm free. Free to love you with all my heart and soul."

"That's wonderful, Sara!"

But then another doubt crept into her mind. She laid a hand on his arm. "What about your feelings for Cathleen?"

He looked at her with solemn eyes. "A part of me will always care for her. But my heart is big enough for the both of you. You're my here-and-now love. And I do love you, so very much!"

"Do you forgive me for deceiving you all those months?"

He nodded. "I probably would have done the same thing in your situation. But what about me being like your father? I remember how angry you were when I made your appointment with the hypnotist."

"You're not like him at all. You truly wanted to help me, not control me. And you were supportive of my interest in baking. My father never would have given me the encouragement you did."

"I'm glad you see us as individuals. I promise I'll never try to control you, either. If I do, give me a slap, will you?"

Relief flooded her, and she grinned. "Agreed."

He put his arms around her. His gaze lowered to her mouth. Anticipating his kiss, she leaned into him and parted her lips. In the next moment, his mouth closed over hers. The kiss began gently but soon escalated into one full of intensity and passion.

Ignoring the amused glances of passersby, Sara kissed him back with all her heart. Happiness filled her. Now she was whole and complete.

A voice over the loudspeaker boomed, "Train now boarding for Denver and all points west. All aboard!"

Sara reluctantly broke away from Jackson. "That's my train."

"Our train," he reminded her.

"Are you going all the way to California with me?"

"Of course. Do you think I'd let you out of my sight when we've just found each other again? No way. I'll change my ticket when we get to Denver."

He rose and held out his hand. "Come on, love. From now on, we're together."

Epilogue

Two months later

"The christening was lovely," Sara told Molly.

"Yes, it was." Molly shifted little Karleen Sara from one shoulder to the other.

"Her outfit is sweet." Sara reached up to touch the delicate, lacy headband encircling the baby's head, then the matching lace on her long, white dress. The baby smiled and gurgled.

They stood in the yard of the Rolling R, where Sara and Jackson were hosting a christening party for the Drakes. Although new snow dusted the mountain peaks and the leaves were beginning to turn, the October day was warm enough for an outdoor party. Fifty guests were present, many of them relatives of Buck's and Molly's. Some had traveled from out-of-state to attend the ceremony held earlier at a church in Red Rock.

Molly said, "I can't tell you how thrilled we are to have you and Jackson as Karli's godparents. I know she'll grow to love you as we do."

"We are honored, Molly," Sara said as they began a leisurely stroll. "I'm so glad you could postpone the ceremony until Jackson and I returned from our wedding trip. And thanks for understanding about my deception. Everyone here has been so kind to me."

"No problem," Molly said. "We're all happy things worked out for you two."

"Me, too, needless to say." She stopped and looked around. "Where is my darling husband, anyway?"

"Over there, talking to Dr. Mike." Molly nodded toward the porch.

When her gaze landed on Jackson, Sara's heart swelled with love. He looked gorgeous in his white, western-style shirt and brown slacks, every bit as handsome as on their wedding day. They'd been married in a quiet ceremony in the redwood forest of California. She would love him with all her heart for the rest of her life.

"I'm glad Rose was able to get time off to come today." Molly captured Sara's attention again. "Wouldn't it be great if she and Dr. Mike got together again?"

"Yes, but it doesn't seem likely. Whenever they're in each other's company, they say hello, then spend the rest of the time avoiding each other like the plague. Do you know what the problem is between them?"

Molly shook her head. "No one else seems to know, either."

Buck joined them. "Can I have Karli for a while? Aunt Nettie wants to hold her."

"Sure." Molly transferred the baby to her husband's waiting arms.

"Come on, little darlin'." Buck planted a kiss on Molly's cheek before walking away.

Molly looked after her husband with a smile on her lips. "He's a wonderful father."

"Yes, you're lucky."

Molly turned back to her. "Jackson will be, too."

Sara nodded. "I'm glad our children will have a better father than I did. What my father did was inexcusable."

Molly's brow wrinkled. "Maybe in time you'll be able to have a relationship with him again. On your terms, of course. But don't give up."

"That's what Jackson says. And, although Dad's

still furious with me for leaving again, he didn't try to stop me from having my horse, Marco, brought here."

"Marco's a beauty. He's a great addition to Jackson's stable. But, what are your plans? Jackson told Buck something about you starting your own business."

Excitement bubbled up in Sara. "I'm considering starting a commercial baking operation. When Jackson told me the Golden Baking Company wanted my cookie recipe, I thought, why don't I start my own company and make them myself? Put my trust fund to a good use."

"Sounds like a wonderful idea."

Several other guests joined them. Sara was deep in conversation with high school friends of Molly's when someone tapped her on the shoulder. She turned around to see Jackson.

"Say, love, can you spare me a minute?" His warm breath tickled her ear.

"Why, sure." She turned to the others and excused herself.

He took her hand and led her down the path toward the barn, then stopped under the apple tree.

"Is anything wrong?" she asked.

"Yes." His eyes twinkled. "I haven't had you to myself all afternoon." He wrapped his arms around her and pulled her close.

Secretly elated, she reached up and clasped her hands around his neck, admiring her rings as they sparkled in the sunlight. "But we're hosting a party."

"The party's great, but I'll be glad when everyone leaves and we're alone." He nuzzled her neck. "There are so many things I want to tell you."

His lips sent little tingles of desire all the way down to her toes. "There are still things you haven't told me?" she teased back.

"You're already tired hearing me say, 'I love

you'?"

"Never. And I love you, my wonderful husband."

He reached up to caress her cheek. "As soon as everyone's gone, I'll take you upstairs and show you just how much you mean to me."

Images of the delicious lovemaking they'd enjoyed since their wedding flashed through Sara's mind, along with a surge of desire for what was yet to come. "I can hardly wait."

"Here's a little sample, to keep you until then."

"Until then," she said, and lifted her face for his kiss. How lucky she was—a dash across the country led her to the one person who helped her discover herself.

SARA'S PEPPERMINT DREAMS COOKIES
½ cup softened butter or margarine
½ cup sugar
1 egg, beaten
2 cups flour
¼ tsp salt
1 tsp baking powder
1/3 cup milk
1 tsp peppermint extract
1 cup crushed peppermint candy
1 cup chopped nuts

Blend butter and sugar. Add beaten egg. Sift flour, salt, and baking powder together and add alternately with the milk and peppermint extract. Fold in the candy and nuts. Drop by teaspoons onto greased cookie sheet and flatten. Bake at 350 degrees for 10 to 15 minutes. Makes approximately 3 dozen cookies 2 inches in diameter.

Thank you for purchasing this Wild Rose Press publication. For other wonderful stories of romance, please visit our on-line bookstore at www.thewildrosepress.com.

For questions or more information contact us at info@thewildrosepress.com.

The Wild Rose Press
www.TheWildRosePress.com

Printed in the United States
133636LV00001B/3/P

9 781601 543851